## "You sure know how to cheer someone up."

She snuggled the dog against her cheek. The poodle licked a tear from her face, her tongue tickling Kathleen.

"So I see you're happy a[illegible] said behind her.



"If I tell you I am, y[illegible] and you won't be ab[illegible] hat."

"I'll get a bigger size." He smiled. "Let's walk her and introduce her to the Soaring S."

Kathleen allowed him to draw her to her feet, only inches separating them.

His heartbeat kicked up a notch and all he could think about was holding her. But that would take them in a direction they shouldn't go. She needed to figure out what she wanted. He did, too.

He took her hand. In the darkness he didn't want her to stumble. That was the only reason.

*Yeah, right.*

He would support Kathleen, be there for her, help her. But he wouldn't fall for her.

If only it was that easy....

**Books by Margaret Daley**

Love Inspired

*Gold in the Fire*
**A Mother for Cindy*
**Light in the Storm*
*The Cinderella Plan*
**When Dreams Come True*
*Hearts on the Line*
**Tidings of Joy*
*Heart of the Amazon*
†*Once Upon a Family*
†*Heart of the Family*
†*Family Ever After*
*A Texas Thanksgiving*
†*Second Chance Family*
†*Together for the Holidays*
††*Love Lessons*
††*Heart of a Cowboy*
††*A Daughter for Christmas*
***His Holiday Family*
***A Love Rekindled*
***A Mom's New Start*
§§*Healing Hearts*
§§*Her Holiday Hero*
§§*Her Hometown Hero*

Love Inspired Suspense

*So Dark the Night*
*Vanished*
*Buried Secrets*
*Don't Look Back*
*Forsaken Canyon*
*What Sarah Saw*
*Poisoned Secrets*
*Cowboy Protector*
*Christmas Peril*
"Merry Mayhem"
§*Christmas Bodyguard*
*Trail of Lies*
§*Protecting Her Own*
§*Hidden in the Everglades*
§*Christmas Stalking*
*Detection Mission*
§*Guarding the Witness*
*The Baby Rescue*
*Bodyguard Reunion*

*The Ladies of Sweetwater Lake
†Fostered by Love
††Helping Hands Homeschooling
**A Town Called Hope
§Guardians, Inc.
§§Caring Canines

***MARGARET DALEY***

feels she has been blessed. She has been married more than thirty years to her husband, Mike, whom she met in college. He is a terrific support and her best friend. They have one son, Shaun. Margaret has been writing for many years and loves to tell a story. When she was a little girl, she would play with her dolls and make up stories about their lives. Now she writes these stories down. She especially enjoys weaving stories about families and how faith in God can sustain a person when things get tough. When she isn't writing, she is fortunate to be a teacher for students with special needs. Margaret has taught for more than twenty years and loves working with her students. She has also been a Special Olympics coach and has participated in many sports with her students.

# Her Hometown Hero

## Margaret Daley

Recycling programs for this product may not exist in your area.

ISBN-13: 978-0-373-81787-0

HER HOMETOWN HERO



This edition published by arrangement with Love Inspired Books.



www.Harlequin.com

**Printed in U.S.A.**

The Lord will give strength unto his people;
the Lord will bless his people with peace.
—*Psalms* 29:11

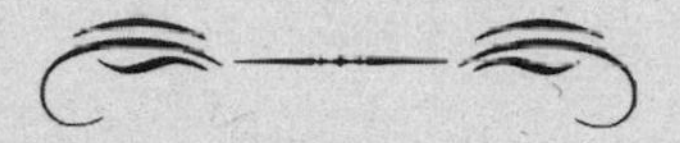

To my family. I love you.

# *Chapter One*

Coming home should be filled with joy, but Kathleen Somers felt nothing. Numb, she was beyond caring where she lived so long as she could be by herself. She stared unseeing out the window of her older brother's Ford F-150 as Howard turned into the family ranch outside of Cimarron City, Oklahoma. Green pastures were scattered with cattle grazing peacefully, their world not rocked like hers. *To my very foundation,* whispered through her thoughts.

In New York she'd been following her dream to become a principal ballerina in a major ballet company. She'd been close—a step away until she was hit by a car crossing the street on her way to the dress rehearsal for her big chance. As she remembered, her heartbeat slowed to a painful throb.

The motion of the Ford came to a halt. "We're

home, Kit," her brother's deep gravelly voice pierced through the emotions deluging her. "Beth hoped you would join us for an early dinner before going to the cabin."

Kathleen slowly opened her eyes, not used to hearing her old nickname. In New York she was Kathleen, and it seemed to fit a ballerina who was on the rise in the dance world. She turned her head toward Howard. "I'd rather settle in first."

"That's fine. We can hold dinner. Give you the time you need."

"I don't think—"

"I know you're hurting, but Beth has gone to a lot of trouble to make one of your favorite foods, and the kids are excited to see you again." His eyes softened on her face. "Please."

"I don't want any special treatment. I'm tired..." Her voice trailed off into the silence when she took in her brother's worried expression. "I'm going to be all right." *If I say it enough, maybe it will happen.*

"Don't forget I've known you ever since you were born twenty-six years ago. I know all your moods and probably what you're thinking right now."

Why had she decided to come home to the Soaring S Ranch? She should have known Howard would do this. Demand she become part of the family when all she wanted to do was hide and mourn the loss of the lower part of her leg—not to mention her career and her dreams. “Fine. I’ll come for a little while, but I really am tired and want to go to bed early. I’ll come up to the house after I freshen up.”

“Promise?” Determination mixed with the concern in Howard’s gray eyes.

She knew that look. He would get his way somehow. Anger seeped into the numbness. “I said I would.”

He grinned, purposefully ignoring the frown on her face. “Good.”

After restarting the truck, he backed away from the house and continued on the road toward the black barn. Kathleen’s gaze latched on to a new shiny red pickup parked by the paddock on the right side.

“Did Bud finally get a new pickup?” Howard’s foreman had needed a new truck for years, but somehow this vehicle didn’t seem his style.

“Nah, he’s still set in his ways and refuses to get a new truck. That’s the vet’s. He’s here checking on Cinnamon.”

She looked toward Howard. “What’s wrong with my horse?”

“Colic.”

“Is it serious?”

“I’ll know after he checks her out.”

"Why didn't you tell me?"

"Because I wanted to get the diagnosis first. But for what it's worth, I don't think she's in extreme pain." Howard steered around the curve in the road.

That was when she saw the cabin. It stood a hundred feet away on the opposite side of the road from the barn, nestled among a yardful of flowers in bloom that her grandmother had loved to tend to. Childhood memories flooded her of spending time at the two-bedroom log cabin with her grandparents. She remembered helping Granny plant her garden out back every year, then picking the vegetables at the right time, often eating a few before taking them inside for her grandmother. The house had been empty since Granny died three years ago, not long after her grandpa had passed away and her mother had remarried and moved to Arizona.

She pushed away that sad memory of losing her grandmother and concentrated on the riot of different colored roses along the front of the cabin. Red, yellow and pink ones swayed in the breeze as though waving a welcome. "You all must be having a warm spring. The roses are blooming early. I didn't usually see them this full-blown until the end of May."

"Yes, which probably means a hot summer."

Howard pulled up to the cabin and switched the engine off.

"It wouldn't be Oklahoma without a hot summer." Kathleen pushed open the truck door and started to exit.

"Hold it. I'll help you down."

She swiveled around. "No. I can do this. I'm not an invalid." She hated that word and was determined to take care of herself.

Her brother's face tensed. "I didn't say that. It's a big step, you're petite and you said yourself that you're still getting used to your artificial leg."

She didn't respond to him, but instead scooted to the edge and put her good leg on the running board, then eased out of the cab to the ground, clutching the door for support. As she made her way toward the porch steps, Howard hovered nearby, one of her suitcases in his hand. Being tall and lanky, he had to slow his normally fast pace.

She glanced at the two rocking chairs with a white wicker table between them to the right. To the left was the porch swing. Many evenings she used to sit with Granny and talk about her day. She'd tell her any problems she had, and her grandmother would give her advice or her opinion. Over the years Kathleen had grown to realize Granny was a very wise woman. She had also been full of faith—a faith Kathleen was no longer certain she shared. Where was the Lord now when she needed Him the most?

*Nothing is impossible for the Lord.* Granny's words taunted her when contrasted with the impossibility of Kathleen being able to dance again.

Howard opened the front door, a wooden one carved by her grandfather not long before he passed away. Kathleen moved inside, her fingers tracing the grooves in the piece of oak that formed a picture of horses grazing in a pasture. A work of art to match the carving of the rearing stallion in front of the main house.

A few feet inside, she paused and scanned the familiar surroundings. A warm chocolate-brown leather couch and two lounge chairs were grouped around a wood-and-glass coffee table on the right side of the cabin. To the left was a full kitchen separated from the dining area by a counter with four stools. On its beige ceramic countertop sat a bouquet of fresh flowers.

"I see Beth has been here." Kathleen took a deep breath of the fresh air laced with the scents of apples and cinnamon as if her grandmother had just removed one of her special pies from the oven and was letting it cool on the stove top.

"She wanted to make sure everything was clean for your return."

"I don't want you all to go to any trouble for me. I can take care of myself."

"I know that. We would have done the same thing for anyone staying here after it has been closed up for three years."

"Who tends to the gardens out front?"

"Bud. Granny was like a second mother to him. He knows how much the gardens meant to her." Howard placed the suitcase on the floor. "I'll bring in the rest of your luggage. Are you having things from your apartment shipped here?"

"No." She kept her back to him as she walked toward the hallway that led to the two bedrooms and bath. "I sublet my apartment furnished, and then sold or gave away everything else except what is in my three suitcases."

"Kit—"

She stopped and glanced back at her brother. "Don't say it. I don't need any reminders of my life in New York."

"But you kept your apartment."

"As an investment for the time being."

"Are you sure that's the only reason?"

"Yes." She frowned. "What else could it be?"

"Not moving on. You're keeping that tie to New York."

She lifted her chin. "Because I might go back one day? I might…" What? Return to her career? Emotions crammed her throat, and she couldn't continue.

Sorrow in his eyes, Howard took a step toward her.

She held up her hand to stop him, shaking her head. If he hugged her at this moment, she would fall apart.

He respected her request, but still said, "I'm here for you," before he pivoted and left the cabin.

She'd hurt his feeling by not letting him comfort her, but she couldn't deal with it at the moment. This was all so hard on her. Leaving the life she'd had in New York. Getting on the plane this morning. Landing here. Coming to the ranch, the place where her dream had begun.

With a deep sigh, Kathleen continued her trek to the bedroom she used to use when she slept over at Granny's. That was the one she would continue to use now, although the other room was a lot bigger. Pausing in the doorway, she took in the double-size brass bed with one end table and lamp beside it. The only other pieces of furniture were a six-drawer dresser and a Queen Anne chair of rose brocade that blended with the flowered coverlet on the bed.

Home. She suddenly felt more at home here than she had in the six years she'd lived in New York City. The feeling took her by surprise.

"Where do you want me to put these?" Howard asked behind her in the hallway.

"In here."

"Why not the larger bedroom?"

"That will always be Papa Keith and Granny's room to me. This is mine." She ignored the ache in her leg and crossed to the bed to hoist the piece of luggage she carried. "When do you need me at the main house?"

"Will an hour be long enough?"

She nodded and opened her first suitcase. Whenever she traveled, she always liked to put her clothes and belongings away before doing whatever else she had to do. It gave her a settled feeling and right now she needed that.

"See you then. Carrie and Jacob are excited about you being here. Coming home at Christmas just isn't enough for them, especially Carrie. You know that she wants to be you one day."

*Not anymore if she knew what happened to her.* Carrie's budding love of dance, much like hers at an early age, had been a bond between them even from a distance. The loss of the connection from their shared dreams was just one more thing the accident had taken away from her.

She opened her mouth to say something to her brother, but he was already gone. Her shoulders sagging, she sank onto the bed to rest a moment.

She loved her niece and nephew, but she wasn't sure about seeing them and answering all the questions they most likely would pepper her with. They were curious and would want to know everything about what happened four months ago. They knew she'd had an accident but from what Howard had said, it was clear that they didn't know she'd lost her leg. She would give them just enough information without a lot of detail or she would never be able to end the evening at a reasonable hour. She was thankful they would be going to school for at least a few more weeks. That would give her the time to decide if she wanted to stay or…

Or nothing. She was adrift, going wherever the current took her. No plans. No goals. So different from what she was used to, and what she needed in her life—a direction. She'd always had one—her dream to dance. The settlement from the insurance company of the man who had hit her allowed her to be financially solvent, and she was thankful for that, but the accident left a void she wasn't sure she could ever fill.

She blew a breath of air out through pursed lips, then set about emptying her suitcases. For the time being, she stored her luggage in the closet in the other bedroom. When she glanced at the clock on the oven, she was surprised she still had thirty minutes. She was tired and could lie down for fifteen minutes, but she was afraid she would go to sleep. Maybe she'd check on Cinnamon before heading for the main house. She hoped the vet was gone and no one was in the barn. Dr. Harris had been their vet for as long as she could remember, and she felt good that her quarter horse was in his capable hands. But that didn't mean she wanted to make conversation—with the doctor or with anyone else.

As Nate Sterling walked through the barn, he couldn't stop thinking of the glimpse he'd gotten of Kit entering the cabin thirty minutes ago. Beth had told him she was coming to stay for a while, but it had still been jarring to see her. Kit's sister-in-law had mentioned Kit had been injured and was recuperating here. He couldn't see her staying long. Her life was in New York. He'd discovered that the painful way when Kit chose to pursue her career over marrying him. His love hadn't been enough.

Reaching the doorway of the barn, he looked over to the cabin's porch. He hadn't seen her in years and yet physically she hadn't changed. Her reddish brown hair was still long and pulled back in a ponytail, her favorite way to wear it unless she was dancing, then it was in a bun. He loved it when she let it down loose, a mass of curls about her face and shoulders. The memory of running his fingers through the thick strands made him clench his hand. He shoved the memory away.

But another image flooded him. Kit the last time he saw her, with excitement on her face from the news she'd received about being accepted into a New York ballet company. Her large, expressive blue eyes, fringed in long dark lashes, lit with a look he'd wished had been for him. That was when he knew even if he'd transferred to New York for college, it wouldn't work.

"How's Cinnamon?" a gruff voice asked behind Nate.

He tore his gaze away from the cabin and swung around to face Bud, the ranch's foreman. "She should recover fine. I see Kit arrived."

"Yeah, Howard and Beth have been working for days on the cabin to get it ready." Bud's sharp regard studied Nate.

Bud had come upon Nate not long after he and Kit had parted all those years ago at Christmas. Nate had ridden back to this barn while Kit had stayed up on the rise that overlooked the ranch. The older man had taken one look at Nate's face and immediately asked if everything was all right.

Nate hadn't said anything to Bud about breaking up with Kit that day, but later Bud had told him any time Nate wanted to talk, he was a good listener.

"Do you think she'll stay long?" Nate finally asked the question nagging at him. He spent time at the Soaring S Ranch, taking care of the animals and renewing his friendship with Howard and Beth. He enjoyed his visits, but the thought of crossing paths repeatedly with his ex-girlfriend made him uncomfortable.

"Don't rightly know. That, you'll have to ask Kit."

"Probably not. She never stays away from the dance world for long. Can't, if she wants to stay on top." For a moment Nate remembered how football had been for him in high school and college, at times taking over his life. "It's like a football player training for the Super Bowl. It's a nonstop process if you want to succeed, and if there's anything I know about Kit, it's that she likes to succeed and do her best." Like him, except football hadn't been his dream but his dad's as a means to pay for college.

Bud's craggy features split in a wide grin, the grooves on his tanned face deepening. "Yeah, that's my gal."

"Then why is she here? The spring season

hasn't ended for her ballet company. Why come all the way to the ranch for a short recovery?"

Bud's bushy eyebrows hiked up. "You don't know?"

Nate shook his head.

"The recovery isn't as short as all that. She was injured four months ago."

Four months and she still hadn't recovered? Then the injury was more involved than Beth had led him to believe. For a few seconds he wondered if Kit might be back for good. Hope flared for an instant, only to be iced over with dashed dreams. She'd been injured before and went back to dancing—every time.

Nate released a long breath. "I'd better make sure Cinnamon is still all right."

"Yeah, I totally agree. I'm sure Kit will want to ride Cinnamon as soon as possible. She always does when she comes home to visit." Bud bent over and lifted a bale of hay, then sauntered toward the last stall.

Nate threw a glance over his shoulder toward the cabin. Would he see her again tonight? *And why do I care? She's made it clear that all we could ever be is friends because her life is dance.*

When Kathleen stepped out onto the porch, she took a deep breath, the scent of mowed grass and roses from the multitude of bushes comforted her. She'd forgotten how much she missed this place, especially the horses. She'd missed Cinnamon. Hopefully the mare wasn't dangerously ill. Although her brother didn't seem to think it was anything serious, she needed to hear the diagnosis from Dr. Harris.

Noticing the red truck still parked near the paddock, Kathleen made her way toward the barn. When she entered the large black structure, where she'd spent many hours as a child, it took a few seconds for her eyes to adjust to the dimmer light. Unless Howard moved Cinnamon, the mare usually stayed in the second-to-last stall on the right when she wasn't in the pasture. Kathleen headed toward the stall, limping slightly, her leg throbbing. The day's travel had been hard on her injury. She'd use that as a reason to cut the evening short.

A large man, dressed in jeans and a long-sleeve, light blue shirt backed out of the stall, grasping a brown bag. Beneath a tan cowboy hat, dark, almost black, hair curled at the top of his collar. With broad shoulders and slim waist and hips, the man wasn't Dr. Harris. She halted. Something was familiar about the guy with his back to her.

Then he turned toward her.

Nate Sterling. Her high school sweetheart—

until he went away to college and she left to pursue a career as a ballerina.

She swallowed her gasp as his soft, gray gaze settled on her. The corners of his eyes crinkled with a smile lighting his features. For a few seconds she was whisked back to eight years ago when she'd said goodbye to him. He was a year older than her and had been a sophomore at Auburn in Alabama, where he was attending on a football scholarship.

The long distance hurt their budding romance. The summer after she'd graduated from high school, she'd left Cimarron City for San Francisco to be part of a ballet company, and they'd drifted further apart over the months. When she was offered a position in a corps de ballet for a New York company, she'd told him it wasn't working and they needed to cut their ties all together. Worrying about their relationship drew her focus away from her dancing. New York was her big chance. She needed to concentrate on her career while she was young, not on a man over halfway across the country.

"Hi, Kit. I heard you were coming home."

Her throat closed, the sound of his deep husky voice shivering down her spine. In the years they had been apart, it had grown huskier and deeper. Nate was also taller than he'd been by at least a couple of inches. He must be almost six and a half feet. His features—an aquiline nose, high cheekbones, square jaw—were sharper. Clearing her throat, she forced herself to speak. "You're a vet now? I thought you were thinking about medical school."

"In high school, sure. But during my sophomore year in college, I realized I wanted to treat animals, come back here."

Whereas Cimarron City could never offer her what she wanted. "Oh," she murmured, pressing her lips together, trying to remember if he had ever told her about his changed plans. By then they were only talking a couple of times a week that soon turned into only once a week. By Christmas of his sophomore year, she'd known it was over. She'd figured he felt the same way. He'd been troubled and not his usual self and for the first time in their relationship, not communicative. They had been going in opposite directions ever since she'd graduated from high school and become focused totally on her career.

He seemed to be waiting for her to reply. She needed to say something or go. The urge to escape was strong, especially when his gaze brushed down her length. Did he know about her leg? She'd asked Howard not to tell others in town, and with long pants it was easy enough to hide her deformity. "How's Cinnamon doing?"

she finally inquired, needing to ask about her horse before departing.

"I can treat her colic with antibiotics. She should be better in a few days. I'll come back and check on her, but you should be able to ride her by next week."

"Oh, good." She concentrated on walking without limping toward the stall. She wasn't ready to answer a thousand questions concerning her injury and her leg. But the act of doing that caused her leg to ache even more.

Nate sidled away to allow her to look into the stall where Cinnamon stood. The quarter horse neighed at the sight of her and came to the door, nudging Kathleen with her head. She stroked Cinnamon, her coat reddish-brown—similar to Kathleen's own hair color. That was what had drawn her to the filly when she was born on the ranch twelve years ago. When she wasn't dancing, she had been riding. Those had been her two favorite activities as a teen. She couldn't dance anymore, but she should be able to ride. The thought boosted her spirits.

"I'll be back tomorrow to check on you, girl." She rubbed her hand down the white blotch on the mare's nose, then blew her a kiss, something she had done from the very beginning whenever she was leaving Cinnamon.

Kathleen rotated toward Nate, her mouth lifting slightly in a smile. "Are you working with Dr. Harris?"

"Yes, I'm his new partner. He's great to work with, and his practice keeps expanding. I'm handling all the big animals and the house calls to the ranches."

"Then you must be on the road a lot."

"Usually half my day. We should go out to dinner and catch up while you're still in town. I imagine you won't be staying long. How's your injury? When will you be returning to New York?"

Her chest constricted. Her breath burned her throat. *He knew about her leg?* "My plans aren't settled yet. I'm just focusing on recuperating for now." How much did he know? Surely her brother and Beth wouldn't have betrayed her and told Nate.

"If you want to go to dinner, let me know. You've got to do something while you're here healing."

Something in the tone of his voice indicated he wasn't totally convinced having dinner with her was a good idea, and she had to agree. He was the past, and at the moment she didn't have much of a future.

"My plans are up in the air right now. I just arrived today. I'll call you when I can." Kathleen slowly backed away. She couldn't see him.

He knew her too well. Before they had dated in high school, he'd been her good friend, both of them hanging out with the same crowd. She couldn't take pity, from him or anyone else. That was one of the reasons she'd fled New York. "See you around." She turned and walked as fast as she dared, again putting all her concentration into walking without a slight limp.

She heard Nate call her name, but she kept going, escaping outside. Being around Nate would only bring back those times she'd had a dream to be a ballerina. That dream was shattered now, and she didn't want to be reminded. But as she headed for the main house, she couldn't get him out of her mind. He looked good. Too good for her peace of mind.

At least she had dodged the bullet, as the cliché went. Now that she knew he drove a red Silverado, she would avoid the barn area when he was at the ranch. She would also stress to her brother and his wife that they were not to say anything about her injury, which would only provoke questions about what happened. Questions about the car accident that she wanted so desperately to forget.

She halted at the bottom of the stairs to the two-story house she grew up in and sank down to the second step. She shut her eyes to the ranch about her. Immediately the streets of New York

City filled her mind. With wall-to-wall people jamming the sidewalks, it was difficult to weave her way through the crowd. Noises bombarding her from all angles—horns honking, loud voices, a siren in the distance. But all her focus was on getting to her ballet rehearsal on time, the last one before the opening performance—her big break, something she'd been working years to accomplish. She was starring as the lead in *Wonderland,* a new ballet she'd even helped choreograph. She was ready. She could do it.

Then without checking if the traffic had really stopped, she stepped out into the street when the light indicated she could cross. The sounds of screeching brakes reverberated in her ears as she felt the impact of the truck against her body. Then nothing…until she woke up in the hospital with her left leg amputated from the knee down.

In that instant, her dream died.

## *Chapter Two*

Kathleen stared at the nearby pasture where some mares with their babies grazed. There was something about the scene that eased the sense of panic the flashback to her accident had caused. For the first couple of weeks afterward, she had relived it several times a day. Now it was only every once and a while. Progress.

She grasped on to that and rose. Climbing the stairs to the back deck, she knocked on the sliding glass door to the den, which flowed into the kitchen area and breakfast nook. Beth waved and hurried to let her in.

Before she could step inside, her sister-in-law engulfed her in a hug. "It's great to see you." She moved to the side so Kathleen could enter. "Is everything all right at the cabin?"

"Yes. Thanks for getting it ready and stocking my kitchen." Beth and Nate were the same age and had been friends growing up. In fact, Nate had introduced Beth to Kathleen and later to Howard. As Beth started dating her brother, Kathleen and she had become good friends.

"You haven't said anything to anyone about what happened to me in New York, have you?"

"No. You asked us not to. I'll respect your wishes, although I don't agree with them." Beth combed her long brown bangs back and hooked them behind her ear, the gesture drawing Kathleen's attention to her sister-in-law's attractive features with green eyes, full lips usually set in a grin and a creamy complexion with a few freckles across her pert nose.

"What do Carrie and Jacob know?"

"I haven't told them anything other than that you're going to be staying here for a while. You said you want to tell them when you're ready." She smiled. "Besides, if I had told them, the whole world would know by now."

"I'll tell them when the time is right." She wasn't sure it ever would be, but she also knew she wouldn't be able to keep the truth from her niece and nephew for long. Maybe soon she would finally get a handle on what she was dealing with. Then she could explain it in a calm voice that would reassure Carrie and Jacob she would be all right.

*But will I be all right?*

She shoved that question away as her niece and nephew ran into the den, saw her and rushed across the room. Kathleen braced herself for their hugs. Before she could say anything, eight-year-old Carrie slowed down as she neared her, but her six-year-old nephew threw himself at her. Beth tried to intervene, but she didn't move fast enough. Kathleen rocked back, the glass door stopping her fall.

"Jacob," Beth shouted. "Is that any way to greet your aunt? Bowl her over?"

With a wide grin, revealing a missing front tooth and sandy-blond hair lying at odd angles, Jacob leaned back, his arms still clasping Kathleen. "Sorry, Aunt Kit. I can't believe you're gonna be here for a while." He crooked his forefinger, signaling she should bend over.

Kathleen did, shifting her weight off her prosthetic leg. "You're growing like a weed. You're going to be taller than me in no time."

Jacob's smile grew. "I'm gonna be like Dad. Big." Then he planted a kiss on her cheek.

Which made up for his overenthusiastic greeting. Kathleen mussed his hair, then held out her arm to draw Carrie to her. "I've missed you two."

"We've missed you," her niece announced. "My birthday will be in two weeks. Are you gonna be here for that?"

"Are you sure, Carrie? Didn't you just have one?" Kathleen teased, knowing how important birthdays in the Somers family were.

"No, I'm positive," Carrie replied in dead seriousness while shaking her head at the same time, her brown-haired pigtails swishing from side to side.

"Well, in that case, I'll put it on my calendar." Kathleen stared into Carrie's cobalt-blue eyes, so similar to hers.

"Okay, kids. Give your aunt some breathing room. You two are supposed to be setting the table. But first wash your hands. So scoot. I'm starved." Beth shooed them away.

As the two children ran out of the room as fast as they'd come in, Howard entered. "I see you're here."

"Don't sound so surprised. I know how to follow directions, and if I'm not mistaken, I was instructed to be here for dinner or you all were going to invade my home."

Howard harrumphed. "You may know how to follow directions, but that doesn't mean you do. Don't forget I know you well."

"Yes, yes. For twenty-six years as you informed me earlier." Kathleen ignored her brother and swung her attention to Beth. "Can I help you?"

The doorbell rang.

Carrie yelled from the front of the house. "I'll get it."

"Me, too," Jacob chimed in, even louder than his sister.

"I fear for whoever is at the door." Kathleen started toward the kitchen with Beth. "Are you expecting anyone?"

Beth stopped in her path. "Since you mentioned it—"

"Dad, Mom, Dr. Nate's here," Carrie announced for the whole ranch's benefit a second before Nate made his way into the den.

Kathleen's gaze locked with his, her heartbeat reacting with a faster tempo. Seeing him at the barn was all she could handle for her first day back home. He'd always been so perceptive. He'd figure out how serious her injury really was if he was around her for too long.

"Nate is coming to dinner, too," Beth finished.

A room separated Nate and Kit, but he could tell even from a distance something wasn't right with her. He wanted to press her for answers, but it wasn't really his place anymore. They had ended their relationship, not on a bad note exactly, but not a good one, either. He'd loved Kit, but things hadn't worked when they were young.

He'd finally accepted that and moved on. He'd

even dated and become engaged, but in the end he and Rebecca hadn't been right for each other. After a second breakup, he'd decided to pour his energy into establishing himself as a veterinarian and building up his practice with Dr. Harris at Harris Animal Hospital.

Maybe Kit had it right to put her job before all else. He still wished her the best and prayed the Lord filled her life, but after that brief time in the barn, perhaps he should keep his distance. Seeing her again made him think of what could have been. Now it was too late.

Nate plastered a smile on his face and crossed the den. "Cinnamon should be fine, but I'll come again and check on her," he assured Howard.

"That's a relief. With Kit back, I want Cinnamon well." Howard settled his arm over his wife's shoulder. "Are we having dinner soon?"

Beth laughed. "Some things don't change, Kit. Howard still wants his dinner by six. Give me ten minutes to finish up and for the kids to get the table set. It's a nice evening. Why don't you all go out on the deck, and I'll call you when it's ready?"

"Are you sure I can't help you?" Kathleen asked, a reserve in her expression, her chin lifted slightly, her gaze on Howard and Beth as if she was trying to avoid eye contact with Nate.

She was used to performing before thousands

of people, and he was beginning to feel that was what she was doing now. Why? What was going on here?

"I've got everything covered. Go enjoy the gorgeous spring day." Beth scurried toward the kitchen.

Howard slid the door open and swept his arm across his body. "After you two." Once Nate and Kit exited the house, Howard poked his head outside. "I just remembered I have to make a call to the feed store. See you two in a few minutes."

As the door closed, a frown descended over Kit's face.

"We can go back inside," Nate said, watching her usual expressive dark blue eyes dull, her mouth tightening even more. Again he sensed something happened that he was missing. What could be upsetting her? She was injured, but by the way she, her brother and Beth acted it hadn't been that serious. She would spend some time here and return to New York. Why would she be so tense and uneasy over the prospect of a brief visit? Had something else happened—something outside of her injury?

"No, that's fine." She turned around and leaned against the railing, her hands gripping it so hard her knuckles whitened.

"No, it's not. What's going on? You seem upset to be here."

She stiffened, nothing relaxed about her now, although she still tried to appear calm. "Why would I be upset? I'm visiting my family. I have done that periodically. You're the one that hasn't been in Cimarron City."

Her defensive tone put him on alert. He bridged the space between them and sat against the railing, folding his arms over his chest. "I've been here almost a year."

"So you were here last Christmas?"

"I was living here but wasn't in Cimarron City for the holidays. I went to Gulf Shores to be with my mom and dad. It seems you and I keep missing each other." Only confirming in his mind that they were never meant to be together as a couple.

"Two ships passing in the night," she said with a forced chuckle. "I'm surprised Howard and Beth didn't tell me you were back."

"And they didn't tell me you were coming to visit until I showed up today. How long are you going to be here?"

She shrugged her slender shoulder, staring at the pasture beyond the backyard, her profile more angular than he remembered, but her brown hair, with red highlights, pulled back into a ponytail was exactly the same as it had always been.

Frustrated, he released a long breath. “I know we haven’t seen each other in years, but...” But what? They had parted because they weren’t in love enough to put aside their dreams for each other. He’d been trying to play college football, which paid his way through Auburn, and trying to fulfill what his father wanted him to do—go pro when he graduated or become a medical doctor. But in the end neither path had worked for him. By his junior year he could no longer pretend those choices were what he wanted. As for being with Kit...that choice had been taken out of his hands.

Kit slanted a glance toward him. “I’m not who I was.”

“Neither am I.”

“Yeah, you never went pro. In fact, you stopped playing football your senior year.”

“By then I couldn’t juggle the demands of premed and football. I chose my studies over the game.” A game his father had played and in which he had achieved some success as a pro athlete. Dad had been hurt that Nate had not followed in his footsteps. And then when Nate decided to go into veterinary medicine instead of becoming a medical doctor, his dad had been disappointed again in his decision.

"A lot has changed since then for both of us."

The sadness in her eyes touched his heart. He reached out and grazed his forefinger down her arm, the physical contact between them electrifying. "That doesn't mean we can't still be friends. We were once." The words came out of his mouth before he could censor them. Okay, it wasn't that bad. They could be casual friends. Surely he could do that. He'd had over eight years to get over Kit.

Her eyes glistened. "I don't have anything to offer a friend right now. I..." She shook her head. "Tell Howard and Beth I'll talk to them tomorrow morning. I'm going to have to skip dinner. I'm too tired from traveling all day." She pivoted and strode toward the steps leading to the yard.

He wanted to go after her, but she'd erected a high wall between them. He knew she was hurting. He just didn't know why. "Don't go. They'll think I drove you away. Did I?"

At the bottom of the stairs, she paused and looked up at him. "No, not really. I just can't do this right now." Then she walked toward the road that led to the cabin.

He started to follow when the sliding glass door opened.

"Where's Kit?" Howard asked.

"Going back to the cabin."

"Why?"

"I'm not sure what happened, but she wanted me to tell you that she was tired and would see you all tomorrow."

"Did she tell you anything else?"

Nate studied his friend's face. "No, not really. Should she have?"

Howard's mouth twisted into a frown. "I had hoped she would."

"What?"

"I can't say. She has to."

"There's something wrong. I knew it. Is it her injury?"

Howard swung around. "Dinner is ready."

Nate gritted his teeth. What were they hiding? He intended to find out. Maybe the injury was worse than she had made it out to be. Had she been asked to leave the New York ballet company since she became hurt in the middle of their spring season? That would bother her since she'd dreamed of working with them above any other dance company. But if that was the case, he was certain she could triumph over the obstacle. When Kit performed, she pulled a person into the ballet story with grace and poise. She had so much to give the world with her abilities. Surely there was another company she could work with, if that was why she was upset.

He told himself it wasn't really his concern.

Whatever was troubling Kit, he was sure she'd find a solution—one that would take her far away from Cimarron City, and back to the world she'd chosen over him.

Having removed her prosthetic leg, Kathleen used her crutches to move around the cabin. She was thankful that Beth had stocked the kitchen, because she was hungry. She'd been looking forward to a good dinner, but had been driven earlier by her wheeling emotions to flee her brother's house. When would she be ready to deal with others? Maybe she would have been better off staying in her apartment in New York, where she could be one of anonymous millions, in a town where she wouldn't have to deal with others' questions.

A moment of madness had prompted her to sublease her apartment for a couple of months and escape to Oklahoma. That, and her brother and Beth hammering at her resolve to stay in New York City. But the main motivator for her to leave had been when her dance buddies began ignoring her wishes to be alone and started dropping by to cheer her up. Nothing they did had worked. She knew she needed a change of scenery. As soon as she'd received the necessary help with her new prosthetic limb and the physical therapy she needed to be able to get around on her own, she'd hopped on a plane. She'd put everything into that, and since she was in good physical shape, she had succeeded quickly.

*Now what do I do?*

Kathleen rummaged in the refrigerator and withdrew some sliced turkey, lettuce and a tomato. As she searched for the bread, a knock sounded at her door. She thought of ignoring it, but when whoever was outside rapped again, she knew she had to answer it and tell the person face-to-face that she was going to bed soon and would talk later.

But when she opened the door, Beth charged into the cabin, carrying a plate wrapped in foil. "I know you're trying to watch what you eat, but I figure you'll get hungry sometime tonight so I brought dinner to you. Fried chicken is good hot or cold."

"I was going to make myself a sandwich."

Beth glanced over her shoulder at the turkey and other fixings on the counter. "Well, now you don't have to. This dinner was made especially for you. I know how much you used to love your mother's fried chicken. Howard tells me I prepare it as good as she does. I consider that a high compliment." She placed the plate on the small dining table and patted her hips. "As you can see, I've enjoyed fixing and eating it often. You could stand to have a little of this fat."

Kathleen stared at her friend, then for the first time in a long while burst out laughing. If she didn't, she might cry. She laughed so hard that tears rolled down her face, and she swiped them away. "I'm not going to blow away."

"Who knows? You know how windy it can get in Oklahoma. What if we have a tornado?"

"I'll join the family in the storm cellar."

"Sit down. Eat. I'll get you some of the tea I fixed for you and put the turkey up. You can have a sandwich tomorrow." Beth did as she said, then joined Kathleen at the table, sitting in the chair next to her. When Kathleen unwrapped the plate and took a bite of the chicken, her friend asked, "What do you think?"

"Delicious, but you don't need me to tell you that. I'm sure my brother has on many occasions. If he hasn't, I'll have a word with him." Kathleen enjoyed some more of the meat, then dove into the baked beans and coleslaw.

"Sorry the baked beans might be a little cold."

"I haven't eaten since I had breakfast at the airport this morning. And this sure beats that meal, even with cold beans."

Beth rubbed her hands together. "I'm gonna fatten you up in no time."

"We'll see about that," Kathleen said when

she finished off the coleslaw. "You know how much I love this. Maybe you can teach me to cook. I guess I have time to learn now. With the company, my schedule was so busy that I usually ate out or had frozen dinners."

"Carrie has been begging me to teach her to cook, too. Maybe I'll work with both of you together. The three Somers girls."

After appeasing her thirst with several large swallows of cold iced tea, Kathleen turned to the fried chicken again. "You don't have to worry about me."

"Why do you say that?"

"Because this is my problem, not yours. I'll overcome it like I have everything." Kathleen tried to put conviction into her voice, but even she heard the flat tone as though there was no life behind the words. "Remember that summer I sprained my ankle? I was back dancing in six weeks."

"This isn't a sprained ankle, Kit. I wish it were. Let me help you." Beth covered Kathleen's hand.

She snatched hers away. "I'm fine. I wish people wouldn't smother me. I'm not like a fragile china doll." *Or am I?* She felt broken like one that had been dropped onto the concrete.

Beth's eyebrows lifted. "Smother you? I'm not doing that. I'm being a caring sister-in-law and friend. That means being there for you—and helping you whether you think you need it or not. And it won't just be me. Lots of people are going to want to help."

"Why would they? No one knows what happened, right?"

"Yes, for now. But you can't keep your injury a secret forever. Nate kept asking us why you were here, how long you would be at the ranch."

"It's none of his business."

"That isn't going to stop him. You two were in love once. I know it didn't work out, but you all were so close in high school—the two of you, and your group of friends. They'll all want to be there for you while you deal with this. Maybe it's time you lean on the Lord, family and friends. There's nothing wrong in doing that. We all need the comfort and strengths of others from time to time. It doesn't mean you're weak."

"You think this is about feeling weak? I don't feel weak as much as lost."

"It's not like your injury is a big secret. It was in the news in New York City."

"A brief mention of a traffic accident buried in the paper. Hardly a big announcement and certainly nothing about my amputation."

"I don't want my children finding out from anyone but you, or at the least Howard and me.

Just so you know everything, Reverend Johnson at church knows."

Shifting toward Beth, Kathleen dropped her fork, and it clanged against her plate. "Reverend Johnson knows about my leg?"

Beth nodded.

"How? Who told him?"

"When Howard found out, he turned to Reverend Johnson for prayer and guidance. He was a big help. He won't say anything, but I think you should at least talk to him. Hiding the seriousness of the injury isn't the answer. You need to accept it and move on. Faith can help you with that."

Kathleen struggled to a stand. Without her prosthetic leg, the movement made her wobble. Leaning into the table, she gripped its edge to hold her upright. "When something like this happens to you, then you can tell me what I need to do. Thank you for the dinner, but I'm exhausted and going to bed." She fumbled for her crutches and positioned them under her armpits.

Painstakingly she hobbled toward the bedroom, weariness blanketing her like a blizzard covering the landscape. She sat on her bed, the sound of the front door closing.

Alone. The silence mocked her. Wasn't this what she'd wanted? A quiet place to think and reflect on what she was going to do for the rest of her life. After laying her crutches on the floor, she fell back on her bed, swung her legs up onto the mattress and stared at the ceiling. She didn't have any answers to her questions, but she didn't have the chance to ponder them for long, either. That last physical exertion whisked her quickly toward sleep.

Nate stared at the computer screen, reading the story in a New York City paper about Kathleen Somers being hit by a car while crossing the street the day before the opening of the first ballet she was starring in. Other than the bare facts, not much else was written about what happened.

He dug deeper until he found another article about Kathleen being replaced in the ballet company by world renowned prima ballerina Rachel LeMasters. So was she out for the rest of the season? Did this mean she was out of the ballet company for good? Was she going to be here longer than a couple of weeks?

He shut his laptop, closed his eyes and imagined her crossing the street, the walk sign indicating it was safe, unaware that it wasn't safe at all. In his mind he saw her being hit, tossed up into the air and landing on the concrete. Limp. Broken. Alone.

He rubbed his knuckles into his eyes, trying to wipe the vision away. His heart pounded a maddeningly quick tempo against his rib cage at the thought of her dreams shattered just before their realization. But that wasn't the case. She was walking about with only a slight limp. Surely she would be back to her old self after she recovered. She'd been hurt before and came back stronger, more determined to prove herself.

The urge to drive to the ranch and demand to see Kit swamped him. He clenched his hands and hammered one fist into the arm of the lounger. If only he'd realized, he wouldn't have insisted to know why she was back in Cimarron City. He wouldn't have pushed to learn how long she was staying—as if he were protecting his own heart. He was vulnerable where Kit was concerned.

It had been hard to walk away from her, but he had realized he was no longer an essential part of her world. He'd never understood her total sacrifice for ballet. He'd been able to walk away from football without a backward glance after working years to excel in the sport.

What worried him the most was that he'd seen a Kit tonight who almost seemed defeated. Feelings stirred deep in his heart. He didn't want to see Kit like that. If she was strong and doing what she loved, then his sacrifice of their relationship all those years ago was for something. If she wasn't with the New York ballet company anymore, then he'd make her see she could be with a different one. She could continue her career after her recovery as she had before. And with her gone from Cimarron City, his heart would be protected.

Barney plopped his head on Nate's arm and turned his soulful dark eyes up at him. "Ready to go for a walk?" Nate asked.

His Great Dane gave one loud bark. Nate needed the fresh air and some exercise while he figured out what he should do about Kit, if anything.

He pushed to his feet and grabbed Barney's leash. When he stepped outside on his porch with his dog, the warm spring air, sprinkled with a hint of rain and blooming flowers, enveloped Nate.

As he walked with Barney, frustration warred with his sympathy and something more elusive. At one time, Kit would have told him immediately about what had happened to her. Finally sadness won out over myriad emotions surging through him. Their relationship had come to secrets and barriers.

When he returned to his house, a teenager stood on his porch, peering into the window to his living room. Barney tugged on the leash, and Nate released his Great Dane.

Steven Case, a large, muscular sixteen-year-old boy Nate worked with in the church youth group, turned at the sound of Barney racing toward him. The teen laughed when Nate's dog pinned him against the window, his big paws perching on Steven's shoulders, and licked him in the face.

Nate mounted the steps to his porch and took a closer look at the boy. Steven was always great with Barney and usually loved seeing him, but tonight Nate glimpsed the tension beneath the boy's demeanor. "Barney, come here." As Nate opened his front door, the Great Dane went inside. "Something's wrong, Steven. What is it?" He leaned against his railing.

Steven stuffed his hands in his jeans' pockets. "I wanted to tell Dad that I didn't want to play football next year. I can't. He'll be so disappointed in me, but I can't take another season. The coach is always on my case. I'm not tough enough. My father wants me to learn how to hit my opponent by taking boxing lessons this summer." He began pacing. "I don't want to hit people."

For different reasons Steven and he had played a game in high school they didn't want to—Steven because he couldn't tell his father how he felt about the sport and Nate because he'd learned football, a game he enjoyed, as a means to go to college. "Do you want me to talk to your dad?"

Steven whirled around, opening and closing his hands at his sides. "No. Don't. He already thinks I'm a wuss. I don't want to make it worse by having someone else handle the hard stuff for me. I shouldn't have come tonight." The teen stormed from the porch.

Nate slapped his palm against the post nearby. He knew better than to make that offer to Steven. First he'd messed up with Kit today and now Steven. At the rate things were going, tomorrow probably wouldn't be any better, because he intended to confront Kit about what was going on.

Kathleen sat at the table, sipping her second cup of coffee and finishing her bagel topped with cream cheese. When she had decided to come to the ranch, she hadn't thought beyond that. But on this first morning, she was faced with what she should do with her time. The insurance company had given her a large settlement to the point where if she invested it properly, she wouldn't have to work ever again. But she would give anything to have her leg back along with her ability to dance.

She glanced at the stack of books she'd put on the coffee table in front of the sofa. She'd never had much time to read and had bought these eight novels, but after that, what?

With her chin resting in her palm, she stared at the clock on the wall over the stove. The second hand going around and around reminded her time kept moving forward, no matter how much she wanted it to go backward. She was almost twenty-seven and had no idea what to do with the rest of her life. She'd always been so busy with work consuming her. Now there was nothing.

She could see if Beth needed any help. Maybe she could ride another horse until Cinnamon was better. Or she could—

A knock interrupted her thoughts. Nine o'clock. Beth had waited longer than Kathleen thought she would when she woke up.

With a sigh, she made her way to the entrance and swung the door wide, ready to launch into all the reasons she wasn't ready to tell everyone about her amputated leg. The plain truth—she just wasn't ready to deal with the fallout of that announcement.

She opened her mouth to speak, but when she saw Nate standing on her porch, she quickly swallowed her words.

She looked Nate up and down, taking in his

jeans, short-sleeve, light green shirt, cowboy boots and hat. He'd always looked good dressed as he was. "What are you doing here?"

His face reflecting a brewing storm, he moved across the threshold without waiting for an invitation from her to come inside.

"We need to talk."

# *Chapter Three*

Did Nate know about her leg? That question flittered through Kathleen's mind as she closed the door behind him, then slowly turned to face him. She squared her shoulders, preparing herself for whatever had put that scowl on his face. It couldn't be good.

"Why didn't you tell me how bad your accident was? You acted like your injury was no big deal. You were hit by a car and then later replaced in your ballet company. That sounds more serious than you implied yesterday."

One sentence after another pelted her as though she were being bombarded with buckshot. For a few seconds a flashback taunted the edges of her mind, but she shut the memories down and focused on Nate standing in front of her. "I prefer not to discuss what happened. I don't owe you an explanation of why I'm here."

Nate blew out a long breath, his scowl dissolving into a neutral expression. "Okay, you're right, but we cared about each other a lot once. I still care. Your dance career is the reason we aren't together today. Will you be able to go back? Is there any way I can help you with your recovery, like I did the time you twisted your ankle?" His look and tone softened.

She balled her hands so tight, her nails dug into her palms. Her wish to be a ballerina wasn't the only reason they'd broken up. Nate had had his own dreams, too. They weren't committed enough to see if they could work their problems out as a team because, although they dated, she had led a very separate life from his. He'd loved sports and had played every one he could fit into his schedule, especially football, which gave him a free ride to college. "There's nothing you can do. I don't need a cheerleader encouraging me to exercise." That was the last thing she needed. It wouldn't take long for him to figure out what her problem was.

"I'm sure you've become quite disciplined over the years to achieve what you have, but it doesn't hurt to let a friend in."

She ignored the last part of his sentence and said, "Yes, I'm very disciplined. I had to be to get where I was."

"Was? Aren't you going back?"

"Dance will always come first in my life." Which was true, but now only as an observer. Averting her head, she moved toward the couch, needing to get off her feet. Her leg ached, although usually each day was slightly better than the one before. "Would you like some tea?"

"You still don't drink coffee?" Nate fit his long length into the chair across from the couch.

She shook her head and made a face. "It tastes nasty, and I still don't understand why you drink it."

"It's an acquired taste."

"One I'll never have." The bantering melted some of the tension gripping Kathleen.

"I'll pass on the tea."

She relaxed against the cushion, hoping they were off the subject of her accident. "Are you out here because an animal is sick? Cinnamon?"

"No. I'm heading to the ranch next to yours, but if you want, I can stop by the barn and see how Cinnamon is doing."

"I'm sure my brother or Bud would call you if there's a problem."

Silence reigned for half a minute while Nate glanced around the cabin. Kathleen frantically searched her mind for something to talk about other than her injury. She wasn't ready to tell anyone about the extent of the damage. She didn't know if she ever would be able to. She was still trying to figure out how to deal with her accident, and it occurred four months ago.

"Why did you decide to settle here?" Nate had come to Cimarron City at the age of fourteen, but before that he'd lived in Alabama—and his parents had returned there several years prior. "I'd thought since you chose to go to Auburn you'd live in that area."

"Dr. Harris gave me an offer I couldn't refuse. Besides, I've always loved it here." He shifted his warm, gray eyes back to her. "I made a lot of friends, and since returning, I've had the opportunity to renew my friendships with many of them."

Whereas she'd largely cut her ties with her friends in Cimarron City. When she had visited at the holidays, she'd only had time for family. She'd thought she had all she needed in New York, but she wondered if she'd really been alone in a crowd of many. She certainly felt that way now. Her friends in New York had the life she wanted and would never have again. It was hard to stand on the outside looking in.

"I'm involved with the youth at church," Nate said when the silence returned. "There are some future ranchers in the group, and we've done some fun activities. Howard has allowed me to use his place for several field trips. We're thinking about having a fund-raiser the third weekend in June at the Soaring S. I could always use your help in the planning. They're raising money for a mission trip to Honduras in August."

"I don't know if I'll be here at that time." She didn't know what she was going to do from one day to the next, let alone over a month away. Before she'd always had a very structured life with everything revolving around ballet. Now she felt as though she were floating aimlessly in outer space with nothing to hold her in place. Even the Lord had abandoned her. All her prayers had fallen on deaf ears.

"That's all right. I can use any help you can give me. I'm desperate. This is the first mission trip I've organized, and I'm feeling a little in over my head." He cocked a grin. "Okay, a lot."

"What made you volunteer for the job?"

"One word—Howard. He heads the youth services at the church, and he recruited me. He thought I would be perfect for the high schoolers."

Her laughter sounded foreign to her ears. "Don't tell my brother, but I agree with him. You will be. How long have you been helping?"

"A couple of months. I casually mentioned to Howard one day that I was thinking of becoming involved more with the church now that I'm settled. I'm warning you—be careful what you say to Howard or there is no telling what you'll be roped into." Merriment danced in his eyes, making them sparkle like polished silver.

"I've been properly warned." The last of her tension slipped from her shoulders. This type of conversation, she could handle.

Nate placed his hands on his thighs and pushed up. "I need to leave. I'll feel better checking on Cinnamon since I'm already here. Walk with me?"

She'd planned to see her mare this morning. Although her leg ached, she wasn't in a lot of pain. The more she walked the faster she would become accustomed to her prosthesis. "Sure." While he headed for the exit, she struggled to a standing position, still not completing that simple action effortlessly.

Turning toward Kit, Nate held the door open for her to exit first, then fell into step beside her. "You never answered me about helping while you're here. It'll give you something to do and, as I said, help a desperate man."

"I hardly think you're desperate. You're one of the most organized people I know. Let me think about it. I just hate committing to too much right now." She couldn't totally stop herself from favoring her injured leg as she strolled toward the barn.

"The youth group is a great bunch of kids—you'll like them."

"I haven't agreed yet. You haven't changed one bit. You can still steamroll a person into doing whatever you want."

"Good. I'm glad to hear I haven't lost my touch. Working with teens is so rewarding."

She shook her head, but a smile tugged at the corners of her mouth. "As I said, let me think about it more than a few minutes. I just got here and haven't even settled in."

"That almost sounds like you'll be here longer than a couple of weeks. How serious is your injury?"

Kathleen gritted her teeth and regretted her comment. It was hard guarding her thoughts and words, especially with Nate, who was perceptive and knew her too well. She didn't have to be so cautious with Howard and Beth and that gave her a sense of freedom. Peering at Nate, she paused under a large oak tree near the barn, not far from the wooden bench under it. Her teeth worried her bottom lip.

His gaze fastened onto the action, and his brow furrowed. "You're not telling me something."

She didn't want to have this conversation. It had been hard enough going through the process of telling Howard and Beth. She'd done that over the phone. Not half a day later her brother had been in her hospital room, ready to whisk her back to Oklahoma. To smother her with the help and attention he thought she needed. The problem was she didn't know what she needed. She'd begged God to show what to do with her life since being a ballerina was no longer an option. She'd had no real choice about keeping her leg, and at the moment she didn't feel she had many choices for her future.

"Your silence doesn't bode well, Kit. Can you continue your career?"

Her throat closed. Emotions she'd tried to keep at bay since she'd returned home surged through her. She now realized leaving New York City had been her first move away from her dream of dancing as a prima ballerina. She'd been so close to reaching the top.

"Now you really have me worried."

She swung her full attention toward Nate. "I didn't ask you to worry about me." *I do enough of that on my own.*

"What's wrong with your leg? You're limping. Will physical therapy help?"

"No…" The words to tell him rose in her, but a knot in her throat kept them inside.

"Have you thought about aqua therapy? I've done some with race horses, and it has been successful."

"It won't make a difference because..." She sucked in a stabilizing breath. "I lost my left leg from the knee down." The last part of the sentence came out in a bare whisper.

But Nate heard.

His eyes grew round, and the color drained from his face. "Why didn't you say something yesterday?" He cleared his throat. "I mean I went on and on about your dancing. If I'd known, I wouldn't have said—"

"Stop right there. I'm not a porcelain china doll that you have to be extra careful with. I don't want your pity."

"And you won't get it." A steel thread strengthened each word. "I know you. If anyone can overcome something like this it's you. I don't pity you, but you can't stop me from caring and being concerned." Again that soft tone entered his voice.

She backed away until she gently bumped against the wooden bench. He closed the distance between them, trapping her. His gaze searched her features, penetratingly intense. She looked away and caught her brother standing in the entrance to the barn, watching them.

A band constricted about her chest as if Nate had roped her. Tears pricked her eyes. "I think you should check on Cinnamon. I'll see her later."

*Please, Lord, help me get back to the cabin*

*without crying. I don't want Nate or my brother to see me have a meltdown. Please. Please give me this.*

"Kit, you aren't alone."

*Yes, I am. I'm the one who has to live with this.* She squeezed past Nate and hobbled as fast as she could toward the cabin, her limp more evident the quicker her pace.

When she reached the safety of her temporary home, she sank onto the nearest chair, and the tears she'd thought she'd conquered swamped her, running down her cheeks.

She didn't know who she was anymore.

A stabbing ache pierced Nate as he watched Kit limp away, but he steeled himself. She'd broken his heart years ago, and he was determined she wouldn't again. But he didn't want to see her like she was—he grappled with the word to describe it. Hurting, yes, but it was much more than that.

*Defeated.*

He'd never seen Kit give up. But they hadn't seen each other in over eight years. He didn't really know her anymore. He'd changed. Grown up. Become more focused on what he wanted. More anchored in his faith. Kit used to be a firm believer. Was she still? She would need the Lord to help her through the adjustments to a new life.

"Give her time," Howard said behind Nate.

He pivoted toward Kit's brother. "Who else knows?"

"Beth and our pastor. The kids don't even know. Kit hasn't accepted it yet. She tells me she has, but she hasn't."

"What can I do?"

"Like I said, give her time. She'll get there eventually."

"Will she be here that long?"

Howard stared past Nate toward the cabin where Kit was and shrugged. "I don't know. I don't think she does, either. But this is the best place for her."

"She'll figure that out." Nate prayed she would. He still cared about her as a friend. "I'm trying to get her to help me with the fund-raiser for the mission trip. Put in a good word for me." Nate began walking toward the barn. "I'll check on Cinnamon and be on my way. But I'm coming back. Kit may not think she needs anyone, but she does."

Howard followed him. "Why are you doing this? You were willing to compromise years ago. She's the one who decided to cut all ties when she moved to New York."

Howard's question stopped Nate in his tracks.

He glanced back at his friend. "I didn't want to leave college to follow her around the country, but I was willing to continue a long-distance relationship. She wasn't, and she was right. It wouldn't have worked in the long run."

"Because her focus was on her career."

"Marriage is hard. If both aren't committed, it won't work." *I don't want to come in second in my wife's life.*

"You can say that again. Beth and I realized that real quickly in our marriage." Howard started for his house where his office was. "You're welcome here any time, Nate. You've got a standing invitation to dinner."

"Thanks, but I actually enjoy cooking at the end of the day. It relaxes me."

"Don't tell Beth. She'll expect me to start helping in the kitchen. That wouldn't be a pretty picture."

Howard's chuckles filled the warm air as he walked away. At the entrance into the barn, Nate peered toward the cabin. The urge to go see how Kit was doing nipped at his good senses, but he refrained. He knew her well enough to realize he had to let her get used to the idea that he was privy to the extent of her injuries.

"Emma, you have a way with animals. What I call a special touch," Nate said to his assistant at the animal hospital, then finished entering notes in a computer file for his last patient, a Great Dane, similar in coloring to his own white-and-black one.

"Dogs are my specialty. Now give me a cat and I'm often at a loss as to why they do the things they do."

Nate laughed. "That's because they have an independent streak with a touch of stubbornness. It's usually their way or no way."

"I do have to admit I've trained a few dogs like that. Some I've given up on. Not all of them can be a service or therapy dog."

He leaned against the counter in the examination room. "I've been thinking about talking to you or Abbey about Caring Canines," he said, referring to the organization that Dr. Harris's daughter, Abbey, had started last year to help supply service and therapy dogs for people who needed them, regardless of their ability to pay. "I have a friend I think who could benefit from a therapy dog."

"What's the problem with your friend?" Emma asked, her long blond hair pulled back in her usual ponytail.

"This isn't common knowledge and must remain between you and me."

"Always. When I train a dog for a person or

someone comes to get one, what information they tell me remains private."

"She lost her leg from the knee down in a car accident and is having a hard time coping."

"No doubt. That can be quite an adjustment. Abbey is working with some veterans who have lost limbs. We've even matched up the ones who want a therapy dog. Nothing beats an animal attuned to your moods, especially when you're depressed. Is she having any nightmares about the accident? Sometimes people will relive the moment their life changed over and over when they sleep. Their subconscious at work."

"I don't know." And he didn't feel he was in a place to ask her—at least not at the moment. For the past two days since Kit had told him, he'd wrestled with what to do about the information, but he knew he had to help her.

"Does your friend have a preference on the breed of dog? Will she talk to me?"

"I'm not even sure if she'll accept a therapy dog, but I have to try. She used to have a black poodle as a kid. Missy went everywhere with her." He could still remember the day Missy died and how hard Kit took it. He'd hurt almost as much as Kit, watching her deal with her grief. When she cared about something, she did deeply.

*Then why couldn't she have cared enough*

*about me?* That question came unbidden into his mind, warning him to be cautious with Kit.

"There's a white, medium-size poodle at Caring Canines I've been working with. I could escalate her training, and she could be available by next week."

"Great. In the meantime I'll talk with Kit about it." He'd have to think carefully about how to approach her so she didn't get her defenses up and refuse. "What's the dog's name?"

"Lexie."

"Okay, then, I'll visit her and see what she says."

"If she doesn't want a poodle, bring her out to Caring Canines. We have several other therapy dogs ready right now."

The receptionist peeped around the door frame. "Your next patient is here."

"Thanks, Caroline. I guess we'd better get back to work," Nate said as Emma made her way into the hallway to bring the next animal back to the examination room.

As Emma led in the next patient, a pet pig, Nate decided to call Howard and invite himself to dinner one evening soon.

Kathleen struggled but managed to secure the saddle on Cinnamon, put the reins over her mare's head and rest the leather straps across her withers. After Kathleen let down the stirrups, she looked to see if anyone else was around the back of the barn where she would mount her horse. Howard had worked with Cinnamon to get her accustomed to being mounted on the right, but this was the first time that Kathleen had ridden her.

Since arriving at the ranch five days before, she'd kept to her cabin. But her brother had come to see her earlier this afternoon and told her about what he'd been doing the past few days since Cinnamon was better. He'd all but challenged her to go for a ride. She'd wanted to but always seemed to come up with a reason not to, even after Cinnamon was over the colic.

What if she couldn't ride with her prosthetic leg? She didn't want to make a fool of herself in front of others. Holding Cinnamon in place in front of her, she stepped up on the mounting block that Howard had adapted with a railing. With a mental count to three, she put her right foot in the stirrup then swung her leg with the prosthesis over the back of her mare and successfully sat on top of her horse. She punched her fist into the air, joy spreading through her.

But when she started out in a walk, her left leg slipped out of the stirrup. Frustrated, she stopped Cinnamon and slid it back into place. She didn't go far from the barn in case there was a problem. Her foot came out a couple of more times until finally she left it out. Her balance was a little off, but she managed to walk Cinnamon around the pasture. Even for a brief moment, she relished the fresh air with the scent of newly mowed grass peppering the light breeze.

When Kathleen glimpsed a red truck drive up the lane—Nate's—she thought about heading for the rolling hills to the east of the house but knew she couldn't avoid him. She made her way back to the barn at a fast walk, her left leg bouncing around more than she liked, which only increased Cinnamon's gait. She hung on and concentrated on keeping her balance. She wanted to dismount before Nate caught sight of her.

*What are you afraid of? He knows. Do you really think you can keep it a secret from everyone for long?* That inner voice that had been nibbling away at her resolve to hide from others kept chipping away at her. What was she going to do, not just for the rest of her life, but right now, the next few weeks? Sit around doing nothing? Maybe ride once a day? Would that be enough?

Kathleen made it to the mounting block as Nate strolled out of the back of the barn and paused near the entrance—watching her.

"Go away," she said, her grip on the reins

tight. Cinnamon tossed her head, and Kathleen loosened her hold.

"I came to see you."

"I'm busy."

"I can wait." He folded his arms across his chest, the brim of his cowboy hat hiding his expression partially.

She drilled her gaze into his, trying to force him to leave. This would be the first time she dismounted with her prosthetic leg. What if she stumbled, fell? She swallowed over and over. "Please."

He strode to her and patted Cinnamon while he looked up at her. "It's okay to need help."

"I need to do this by myself, and I don't want an audience."

"Okay." He pushed his hat off his forehead, revealing his smoky-gray eyes, soft with concern deep in their depths. "I'll be in the barn. Howard is meeting me down here."

"Thanks." She waited until he'd disappeared inside before slipping her right foot out of the stirrup and planting it on the block, and then she swung her left leg over Cinnamon. The past half an hour had drained her energy, and her thigh muscles burned. She sank down onto the piece of wood, holding Cinnamon's reins while she gathered her strength to finish taking care of her mare.

Kit led Cinnamon toward the barn to remove the saddle nearer where it was stored. She heard murmurs as she approached the back entrance.

"Give it a try. It might work," Howard said to Nate as she entered.

"Try what?" Kathleen asked, stopping at the saddle rack.

Her brother shot Nate a look as though to say, *You tell her.*

Nate cleared his cough. "I have a gift for you."

# *Chapter Four*

"I think I hear Beth calling." Howard scurried to the exit, throwing a glance over his shoulder and adding, "Dinner is in an hour. See you *both* up at the house."

Nate wanted to erase the worry in Kit's eyes. "Your brother isn't subtle. He wanted me to meet him down here, but when I asked him why, he didn't have a reason."

"I don't think he knows the definition of *subtle.*" Kit continued her trek across the barn to the saddle rack. "What did you mean you have a gift for me?"

Realizing she might protest, Nate still hurried to help her with removing the saddle. When she allowed him to lift it off and onto the rack, surprise must have graced his features.

"I haven't fully recovered from my accident. I've done too much today."

He took the brush from the shelf nearby and ran it over Cinnamon's coat, keeping a sharp eye out for any outwardly signs of colic. "She looks good. Howard told me she got into a bad batch of feed—that was what had her sick. He threw it out. Thankfully she was the only horse affected."

"I'm glad she's better. It felt good to be riding her again, but it was different. I'm used to using my legs some to control Cinnamon. I'm going to have to modify how I ride and work on building up certain muscles."

"That won't be hard for you. Cinnamon is a good horse and picks things up fast."

"She'll train better than I will."

He slanted a look at her over Cinnamon's rump and saw a grin tilt up the corners of Kit's mouth. "You'll do fine. I've seen you practice a dance move until you did it flawlessly." Her smile faded when he mentioned the word *dance.* "You can't forget what you did for so much of your life. Who's to say you can't do something else involving dance."

She closed her eyes for a long moment, her chest expanding then collapsing before she regarded him again. "You never told me what the gift is that you have for me."

He laughed. "You haven't changed in that department. You always hated not knowing what I was giving you for your birthday or Christmas."

"My birthday isn't for a while, and Christmas is half a year away. I can't wait *that* long."

"You don't have to. I'll have the gift in a couple of days. That is, if you want it."

She lounged against a post nearby while he finished with Cinnamon. "What is it?"

"A poodle named Lexie. She needs a home, and I know how much you loved Missy. She's white and about the same size as Missy."

Her face pale, Kit pushed away from the post. "I don't know about that. I may not be here long."

"That's why I asked Howard if he'd keep Lexie if you left and didn't want to take her with you. He said the kids would love to have another dog."

"I know you're a vet and come into contact with animals that need homes, but why pass her along to me? Why are you doing this?"

"You think I have an ulterior motive?"

"Do you?"

He began walking Cinnamon back to her stall. "Howard wants me to leave her here another night rather than putting her out in the paddock to make sure she's still okay."

Hands on her hips, she scrunched her mouth

into a frown. "Nate Sterling, out with it. Why are you giving me a dog?"

After Cinnamon was safely in her stall, he faced Kit. He couldn't keep from her where Lexie came from, but he'd wanted her to fall in love with the poodle before he told her. "I'm getting her from Caring Canines."

"What's that?"

"Abbey Winters, Dr. Harris's daughter, and his assistant, Emma Tanner, run an organization to help match therapy and service dogs with people who need them."

"I don't need a service dog. I can do for myself."

"I agree."

Her eyes widened. "You think I need a therapy dog!"

"Do you?"

She opened her mouth to say something, but no words came out. Finally she limped toward the front barn doors.

"I never thought you were a chicken," Nate called out from behind her. "I've seen you meet so many challenges head-on. What harm will it do to see if you and Lexie get along? She may be able to help you."

At the entrance, she spun around on her right leg. She wobbled but caught her balance. "How?"

"Comfort you when you need it. Listen to

you. You know how attuned animals are to us. You may not want my help, but take Lexie's." He couched his tone and words into a dare, knowing in the past she couldn't refuse one. "I've talked to many pet owners and so many times they praise how much joy their pets bring to them."

"Okay. I'll try it on one condition. I don't want you to look at me and only see my injury. That's all I got from my dance buddies in New York. Tonight I plan on telling Carrie and Jacob about my leg. I'll have enough to deal with them."

"What makes you think I look at you like that?"

"Because you went to the trouble of getting Lexie for me. I'm not broken. I just need time."

A surge of aggravation flashed through him. He clamped his lips together, trying to choose his words carefully. "I never said you were broken. You did. I've never looked at you like that. An injury isn't what defines a person. How you handle it does."

She glared at him, then turned toward the exit. "Tell my brother I'll be up to the house after dinner to talk with his children. I'm suddenly not hungry."

He wasn't going to let her run away. He

moved quickly and planted himself in her path. “No, *you* tell your brother that. I’m not your messenger.”

“You’re not my friend, either. A friend wouldn’t push me like you are.”

“I hope I have friends who will push me when I need it,” he fired back at her.

She stepped away. “Fine. I’ll call Howard. Be gone by the time I get there.” When she charged toward the cabin, her limp was more pronounced.

Nate deflated. He’d blown it. He’d wanted to shake some sense into her, but he hadn’t handled it at all correctly. When she was forced into a corner, she always came out fighting. Somehow he would find a way to reach her without putting her on the defensive. He might not be able to, but maybe the kids in the youth group could when they come to the ranch tomorrow to plan the fund-raiser. Tonight he’d solicit Howard and Beth to make sure Kit was there when they arrived.

As Kathleen strolled toward the main house, her attention zeroed in on Nate’s truck, parked out front. His red Silverado mocked her order for him to be gone. She came to a halt in the yard, trying to decide what to do.

Beth opened the door and stepped out onto

the porch. When she saw Kathleen, she moved toward her, carrying two mugs. "I was wondering where you were. I made the special tea you like so much."

"Trying to bribe me to stay?"

"Is it working?" Her sister-in-law passed the mug slowly under her nose.

Kathleen drew in the scent of peaches and cream wafting in the heat rising from the cup. "Maybe just a little. Is Nate inside?"

"Nope."

"His truck is here."

"Your powers of observation are sharp." She started toward the house. "Let's sit on the steps. It's been a long day, and I could use the break. And tomorrow will be busy."

"What's going on?"

"We'll have eight teens descend on the ranch. Howard offered this place for the Western Day Fund-raiser next month and the first onsite planning session will be held here."

Kathleen frowned, clasping both hands around the mug and leaning forward. "Nate wants me to help him with the fund-raiser."

"Are you going to?"

"After this afternoon, I shouldn't even consider it." She took a sip and welcomed the smooth taste as it slid down her throat.

"What happened?"

"He thinks I need counseling. He wants me to have a therapy dog."

"That isn't what having a therapy dog means. Abbey started Caring Canines because she has a sister-in-law, a child really, who lost her parents in a plane crash and her legs were injured. The doctors weren't sure if she would walk again even though Madi had several operations to repair the leg. They fixed what they could. The rest depended on physical therapy and the little girl's will. Abbey found a perfect dog to replace the one Madi lost. Her pet died in the crash. Cottonballs was trained to be a therapy dog. It's not like a service animal. Cottonballs helped Madi deal with her injuries, and today Madi runs and plays like anyone her age."

"A therapy dog can't give me back my leg so I can dance."

"No, but you haven't come to terms with that yet. Maybe the dog will help you."

Kathleen's grip around the mug tightened, and she waited half a minute before asking, "How?"

"You can hug and love on her. She'll return the love unconditionally. You can talk to her and she'll listen, but she won't say something you don't want to hear."

"Like you just said to me."

"I've always been up-front with you." Beth

sipped her tea, then set it on the step next to her. "You know my cat, Willie. He listens to me rant and rave about a problem, and by the time I finish talking my way through it, I often have a solution." Her sister-in-law smiled. "And not because Willie told me what to do."

Kathleen put her tea down and shifted toward Beth. "What if I can't figure out what to do?"

"You have me and Howard. I suspect you have Nate, too. He wouldn't have done what he did if he didn't care about you." Beth covered Kathleen's hands with one of hers. "And if you need to talk to a counselor, that is understandable. You've gone through a traumatic ordeal."

"I might not stay here."

"Then you can leave Lexie or you can take her with you. Your choice."

Tears swam in Kathleen's eyes. Had she made a mistake coming home to recover? In New York at least she'd been able to control her see-sawing emotions.

Picking up her cup, Beth rose. "Carrie and Jacob are inside waiting for you. They said something about Jacob challenging you to a game of Memory."

"Where's Nate?"

"Right after dinner he and Howard went to the barn to discuss details about tomorrow. You're safe, at least from him. I can't vouch for my children. They're ready to beat the pants off you."

Gripping the wooden railing, Kathleen heaved herself to a standing position, then bent and grabbed her mug. "They're cutthroat. I beat them yesterday and that's all they've been talking about."

Beth shook her head. "I know. That has to be coming from their dad's side of the family. My side is docile and carefree."

Laughter burst from Kathleen. "I beg your pardon. Who do you think I learned it from?"

Beth tapped her chest. "Me?"

"Right. You."

Beth opened the front door. "I'd better warn you. Carrie has a favor to ask you. If you don't want to, that's okay."

As Beth passed Kathleen to go into the house, she clasped her friend's arm. "What favor?"

"She's auditioning for the Summer Dance Academy, and she wants you to be there."

Suddenly Kathleen was thrown back to her own audition, years ago, for the same program. Madame Zoe, her ballet teacher and mentor, ran it every summer to give children who wanted more intense instruction than during the school year an opportunity to train. "I can't…I…"

Beth turned and embraced Kathleen. "I tried

to discourage her, but she is bound and determined to have you there. You're her inspiration."

The hot ball in her throat made it difficult to swallow. Kathleen finally gulped and murmured, "Not anymore."

Beth pulled back, taking Kathleen's empty mug. "What happened to you doesn't alter that one bit. You don't have to believe me, but Carrie's feelings about her aunt Kit won't change no matter what."

Kathleen smiled to placate Beth, keeping her doubts to herself. "Thanks for the warning. I'll try and think of something to say to let her down gently." Kathleen heard giggles and followed the sound to the den at the back of the house.

When she entered the room, Carrie hid something behind her back. But Kathleen caught a glimpse of what it was. "Are you two ready to get trounced?"

"Are you?" Jacob said, then giggled and covered his mouth.

Carrie punched him in the arm. "He's acting like a dork again." She put on an innocent expression and continued. "Yes, we are. C'mon. I've got the cards laid out in a neat pattern like you taught us." Carrie moved to the side to reveal forty animal cards in eight neat rows, all complete except one.

"One's missing?" Kathleen made her way to the game table and took her seat.

"Oh, no. I still have this to put down." Carrie held up a card with a goat on it. "We can all see where I put it. That's only fair."

"Yeah. The only way to play a game is fairly. Whose turn is it to go first?"

"Mine," Jacob shouted then quickly flipped over two cards—matching penguins. Then he flicked over a pair of cows. When he finally lost his turn, he had five sets of animals.

"My turn." Carrie proceeded to make a few matches, clapping between each one.

"You would think you children have X-ray vision," Kathleen said casually and chose a rabbit and a cat card.

Jacob reached for his first choice.

"Another match. Remarkable." Kathleen looked pointedly at her niece and nephew.

Carrie's mouth turned down in a pout. "Okay. Okay. We knew where the cards were."

"You did?" Kathleen widened her eyes as though she hadn't already known that fact. "That's cheating."

"We weren't cheating. We were playing with ya." Jacob shoved all his cards onto the others on the table.

"Just joking?"

"Yeah," her nephew said, dropping his head.

"For the record I knew you two were up to something. It was written all over your faces. But cheating is when you don't play fairly and don't give everyone the same chance to win."

"You have been so sad lately. We wanted to cheer you up. We were gonna tell you after the game was over, but then Jacob got greedy." Carrie glared at her brother. "We were gonna match just one or two each turn." She waved her hand at his matches strewn over the cards. "Five! You ruined our joke."

Her niece's voice rose the more she talked, but all Kathleen really focused on was the first sentence about her being sad. When she'd visited the ranch in the past, she'd spent a lot of time with Carrie and Jacob. The whole family, her included, went on outings around Cimarron City. But not this time. Clearly the kids had noticed the difference.

"Ouch! You hit me," Jacob yelled.

"No, I didn't. You got in the way of my hand." Carrie pushed her chair back and jumped to her feet.

Kathleen grabbed Jacob before he flew out of his chair and went after his sister. His face red with anger, he plopped against the cushioned back.

"Aunt Kit, she did it on purpose."

Carrie jammed her fisted hand against her

waist. "I talk with my hands like Aunt Kit, and one day I'm gonna be a ballerina just like she is." Her niece stuck her tongue out at Jacob.

*How did this get so out of control?* flashed across Kathleen's mind as she pushed to her feet and planted herself between her niece and nephew. Usually she was more attuned to Carrie and Jacob, but she'd been so absorbed with her situation that she'd neglected them. It was time to make things right.

She placed one arm around each child and said in a soft voice, "Let's sit on the couch and talk. I have something I need to tell you and should have days ago." She still didn't know how she was going to, but keeping it a secret wasn't working, either.

Carrie's forehead crinkled with worry. "I'm sorry. I didn't mean to upset you. Mom said you're still recovering and not to bother you."

Kathleen pulled the eight-year-old against her. "You can bother me anytime. But I will admit I haven't been myself lately." *I'm not sure if I ever will be that person again.* "And the reason for that..." The rest of the sentence lodged in her throat, burning it. *One day I'm gonna be a ballerina just like she is.* Carrie's words robbed her of her voice.

"It's okay, Aunt Kit. We know you hurt your leg, and it'll take time to get better." Carrie threw her arms around Kathleen and gave her a hug. "I love you."

"Me, too." Jacob joined in, forgetting about his fight earlier and embracing his sister as well as Kathleen.

Carrie leaned away. "When you feel like it, we can go riding like we usually do. Go on a picnic. We'll be out of school in two weeks. By then you'll be much better."

Kathleen had known this would be hard, but like with Nate, she hadn't realized how hard. As a ballerina she'd always strived for perfection in her dances. That was how she approached life. But she wasn't perfect. She swallowed over and over, then murmured, "I love you two. I couldn't ask for a better niece or nephew."

Carrie giggled. "Even when we fight?"

"Yes, even then." She kissed the top of each one's head. "This is hard for me, but I have to tell you that I'll never be able to dance again."

Carrie thrust herself back, her eyes round. "Why not? You were injured before and still danced again."

"Because—" Kathleen rolled up her sweatpants to reveal her prosthesis "—I lost the lower part of my leg in the accident."

Jacob's eyes rounded, and he touched her artificial limb. "Cool. How does it work? What's it made from? How long have you had it?"

Kathleen tried to explain the best she could as she showed them how she took it off. Then she put it back on and walked around for them. Carrie remained quiet through the whole demonstration.

"Jacob. Carrie. Time for bed," Beth said as she came into the den.

"Mom, did you see Aunt Kit's new leg?" Jacob pointed to it.

"Yes, I have. You've got the bathroom first, then Carrie. Scoot now." Beth shooed her son out of the room, then followed him into the hallway.

Kathleen silently thanked her sister-in-law. She needed to have a word with Carrie without Jacob around asking questions. "Honey, do you have any questions for me?"

"You can't dance again?" Carrie's voice squeaked out.

A burning sensation infused Kathleen's stomach, and her heart ached. "I can't perform like I used to. But there's more to dancing than that." When she said the last sentence, something clicked inside her. Hope seeded itself in her. "I can still help you when you need it."

"Really? Great, because I want you to come to my audition for the Summer Dance Academy. Just knowing you'll be in the audience will encourage me. There aren't many openings for my age group."

She couldn't run from seeing Madame Zoe, and it was time she faced that. Madame Zoe would be upset if she knew Kathleen was in town and didn't come to see her like she always did. "When is it?"

"Next Saturday, the day before my birthday."

"I'll be there in the audience, cheering you on."

Carrie clasped her and said, "Thank you. Thank you. That's the best birthday gift you can give me."

"So I don't have to go shopping for a present?"

Carrie grinned. "If you want to, I won't complain."

Kathleen winked at her niece. "I figured you wouldn't."

"Carrie. Jacob's out of the bathroom. It's your turn." Beth's shout sounded as if it came from the second-floor landing.

Kathleen hugged Carrie, then walked with her to the entry hall. "See you tomorrow. Tell your mom I'm going to the cabin."

Using a flashlight she'd brought with her, Kathleen made her way to her place. Carrie and Jacob's acceptance and love, coupled with Howard and Beth's, gave her hope she could deal with this and discover something she wanted to do with the rest of her life. But when she thought about things that interested her, they all revolved around dance.

*Lord, I know I haven't prayed to You in a while, but I need You. What can I do? Financially, I don't have to work, but I want to. I need to.*

As she passed the barn she wondered if Nate was with Howard inside. Nate's red truck was still parked in front of the main house. He'd made it easier to talk with Carrie and Jacob since she'd already broken the news about the seriousness of her injury to him. This time wasn't as bad. But she also appreciated his absence when she arrived to see her niece and nephew.

Tomorrow she would apologize for what had transpired in the barn. She knew he meant well.

Kathleen stepped up to the cabin porch. A movement out of the corner of her eye seized her full attention. She swung her flashlight toward the swing at the end and illuminated Nate rising.

# *Chapter Five*

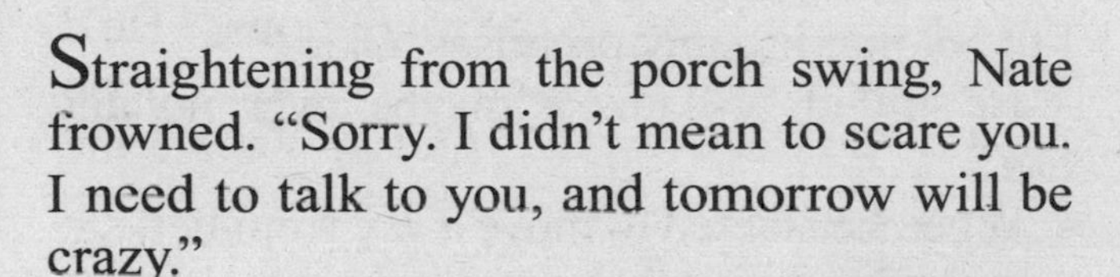

Straightening from the porch swing, Nate frowned. "Sorry. I didn't mean to scare you. I need to talk to you, and tomorrow will be crazy."

Kit dropped the flashlight to her side, a glow from the front window of the cabin giving her enough illumination to follow Nate's progress toward her. "I told the kids tonight. I'm tired."

"It didn't go well?"

"Actually it went better than I'd expected, but I exhausted myself worrying about how they would take it. It's just now hitting me."

He stopped several feet from her, wishing he could erase the tired lines on her face and make everything right for her. "I won't be long then, but I hope you'll come to the barn tomorrow morning around ten to meet some of the kids in the youth group."

She attempted a smile, but it fell short. "You're hoping they'll persuade me to help you."

Although not a question, he said, "Yes. We're trying to come up with something special. Something that hasn't been done in a while. You know how creative I am. On a scale from one to ten on creativity, I'm a zero, whereas you're an eleven."

"Thanks. If you're trying to butter me up, you're doing a good job. I'll try to come, but I'm not making any promises. Okay?"

He smiled. "I'll take a 'maybe' over 'no' any day."

When he started to move away from her, she asked, "Did you and Howard come up with anything?"

"A rodeo was about all, but that has been done to death."

"It's Oklahoma. What do you expcct?"

"Something different but not too complicated."

"I'll think about it. Good night."

He walked a few feet toward the road, then glanced back to watch her go inside the cabin. He was glad Beth had talked him into moving his meeting with Howard tonight to the barn. In the past he would rush in and try to fix things, but with Kit he couldn't push her too hard. Beth made him see that.

Kit would help him, and he would help her. He actually whistled "Oklahoma" as he headed for his truck.

The next morning Kathleen sat at her table, sipping a second cup of Earl Grey tea. She hadn't slept well the night before, her dreams filled with Madame Zoe as she told the woman her star pupil would never dance again. Kathleen knew her mentor wouldn't feel she had let her down, but Kathleen felt that way all the same. It was irrational, but hard to rid her mind of it.

She had purposefully kept her amputated leg from Madame Zoe because it wasn't something she wanted to tell her over the phone when she was in New York or even here at the ranch. But the audition for the Summer Dance Academy in a week wasn't the time or place, either. Early this morning she'd decided she would accompany Carrie to her ballet class and talk with her mentor privately afterward. She didn't want anyone else in town to know until she'd told Madame Zoe on Tuesday.

She glanced at the clock in the kitchen area and realized she was already late for the meeting. Gulping down the lukewarm tea, she rose and crossed to the sink to rinse her cup.

A knock cut into the quietness. As she made

her way to the door, she tried to guess who was sent to get her. When she saw Nate, her heartbeat kicked up a notch, and she felt a smile twitch at the corners of her mouth.

She stepped onto the porch. The spring air held a hint of a chill. Sunlight kissed the plants and animals all around her, beckoning her to enjoy the beautiful day. "I know I'm running a little late. I thought you'd send Carrie or Jacob."

"Why?"

"Because you know I have a hard time saying no to them."

"But you can to me?" A gleam glinted in his gaze.

"You don't have big blue eyes and call me Aunt Kit." She started toward the barn, seeing some teenagers going inside. "How many are going to be here?"

"The fund-raiser committee is four girls and four guys. If the whole group tried to plan this we'd never get anything done."

"Probably a wise decision. What have you all decided so far?"

"To hold the event at the Soaring S and to have a Western theme."

"And it's six weeks away?" Kathleen slowed her gait, her glance sliding to his.

He removed his cowboy hat and raked his fingers through his dark hair. "Yep. Now you see why I'm so desperate. The guys want to do a rodeo and the girls want to do a carnival. No one is budging."

"Both sound good."

"They've both been done in the past few years. I want it to be different." Nate plopped his hat back on his head, pulling it lower to shade his eyes.

"Why?"

"A carnival has been done a lot in the past. We want something a little different. The rodeo is a competition, not to mention possibly dangerous. Some of the kids in the group aren't into rodeo. I'm trying to meld the group together. We'll be together for a week in August in Honduras. I want us to be as close-knit as we can be."

"That makes sense. I might have something."

"What?"

"Let's wait and see what everyone says. There may be a better idea."

When Kathleen went into the barn, she scanned the teenagers, noting all eight were present. Her brother, Beth and Carrie were also in attendance along with Bud. The barn was large but she could understand not having the whole group trying to plan the event. Fourteen was enough, especially when everyone took a seat on a bale of hay and began to talk at the same time.

Nate put his two fingers in his mouth and blew a whistle so loud Kathleen's ear rang for a few seconds.

"Warn me next time you do that," Kathleen said with a chuckle.

"Loud but effective," Nate murmured for her only, as the group quieted. "One person at a time will have the floor. If you want to talk, wait for me to call on you or no one will hear anything. First, I'd like you all to introduce yourselves since we have a newcomer—" he gestured toward her "—Kathleen Somers, Mr. Somers's sister."

"Really?" one red-haired girl squeaked, her eyes saucer round. "I've been taking ballet for ten years. Madame Zoe has one of your photos on the wall in the studio."

Heat scorched Kathleen's cheeks. Everyone stared at her. "Yes, she was my teacher when I lived here. And you are?"

"Oh, I forgot," the teen said, and covered her lips with her fingertips for a few seconds before smiling. "I'm Anna, a huge fan of yours."

Another girl, dressed in an outfit more suited for a runway of high-end clothes, chimed in. "My name is Debra. Where do you dance?"

"I was part of a New York ballet company."

Anna frowned. "Was?"

"I'm recovering from an injury right now."

"We have a lot to do this morning, so let's keep this moving." Nate pointed at the boy next to Anna. "Your turn."

Although Kathleen heard their voices and saw their mouths moving as they talked, she couldn't focus on the introductions and what followed after them. Maybe she'd better go see Madame Zoe this afternoon. The more she was around people, the harder it was to keep her situation a secret.

Fifteen minutes later, the discussion about the fund-raiser had evolved into everyone trying to talk over one another. Nate raised his fingers to his mouth again. Kathleen caught the movement and quickly tugged his arm down, and then she stood.

In almost a whisper she began to talk. "I think we should have a Western hoedown with square dancing, good food and live entertainment."

Anna quieted the kids around her. "Miss Somers, I'm sorry, but I didn't hear everything you said."

When silence dominated the interior of the barn, Kathleen repeated what she'd said. "From what you all have been saying, some of you are musicians and could be the live entertainment, and what person doesn't love good down-home cooking. For the people who don't know how to square dance, we can have instructors to help them learn. You can charge an entrance fee for a night of fun. I think my brother probably can get a wagon or two for hayrides. For the ones who want to ride horses, this ranch has some good mounts."

Bud, the only one who hadn't said a word besides Carrie, raised his hand. "I can be the caller for the square dances."

Everyone in the group nodded their heads and began calling out what they were good at and how they could help.

After another loud whistle, Nate stood. "Thanks, Bud, for volunteering to be the caller. Great idea, Kit. It looks like you all are in agreement. Finally. We'll go with a Western shindig. Debra, would you be our recorder and take down the duties different people volunteer for? We'll need an adult and a teen in charge of entertainment, another pair for food, then also dance and other activities. Once the adults are assigned, the rest of you need to pick what you want to do." He looked around the group and added, "In an orderly fashion."

After Bud and Howard volunteered for the dance and other activities, Beth immediately spoke up for the food.

"Nate and Kit, I guess that leaves you two with entertainment. A show for people who come beyond the dance," Howard said with a twinkle in his eye.

Kathleen leaned close to Nate. "I never said I would be on the committee. I only agreed to come to this meeting."

"That's fine. Do whatever you feel comfortable with, although I have to say we would be a good team with your background in dance and my..." Pure innocence bathed his features.

She fought a grin demanding to be seen. Had he and Howard planned how they were going to persuade her to help with the fund-raiser? "And? What would your contribution be to this—partnership?"

"I'd be great at implementing plans you come up with."

Laughter bubbled up in her. "In other words, you'll be my assistant. I think I like that—that is, if I stay until the fund-raiser date. I might not, you know."

He nodded his head, his gaze trapping her for a long moment. "Duly warned."

She blinked and looked away. Their relationship hadn't worked out in the past, and her life was much more complicated now. What in the world was she doing? Nate's charm had always been enticing to her. The decision to break up with him had been the hardest one she'd ever made.

"I need teen volunteers. You'll be responsible for calling your friends in the group and recruiting more for each of the committees. We'll need a small army to pull this off in six weeks. When you've found six more vict—" Nate coughed "—I mean, volunteers, let me know and also Debra, who will keep track of who is doing what. Okay?"

After the big group broke up into the three smaller ones, Carrie came over to Kathleen. "I want to help you."

"Sure. I'd love your input. People at the fundraiser will be bringing their children. I need to know what would be good entertainment for them and most likely your dad and Bud will need your opinion concerning activities."

"You know Jacob is gonna want to help, too."

"I figured. Where is he?"

"He had baseball practice and couldn't miss it. He can help Dad and Bud."

Nate came up to Carrie and Kathleen. "Let's go outside and find a shady spot to talk about what we should do."

"The bench under the oak tree is a good place." Kathleen wasn't comfortable yet getting up and down from the ground. She still had some issues from a sitting position.

"I'll round up Debra, Anna and Steven and meet you there." Before she moved away, Nate clasped her shoulder and bent toward her. "Save me a seat on the bench. Us old folks have to stay together."

"Old? Speak for yourself," Kathleen said with a chuckle. The whole time every sense was acutely aware of Nate's nearness—sweaty palms, a breathlessness attacking her lungs as if she and Nate were teens again.

Five minutes later when he eased down next to her on the bench while the kids sat on the ground in front of them, she'd wondered how she had found herself in this situation—helping Nate with a fund-raiser that would take a great deal of time. Time she needed to figure out what she was going to do the rest of her life—not be sidetracked by Nate.

"I could have driven myself to see Madame Zoe." Kit sat in the passenger seat in Nate's truck as he pulled onto the highway and headed for Cimarron City later Saturday afternoon.

"No doubt you could, but both Howard and Beth were using their cars and the truck left behind has a manual transmission. If I remember correctly, you had a hard time driving stick years ago. Has that changed?"

"It hasn't," she admitted. "But Beth was going

to be back in a while and she could have taken me or leant me her car."

"Maybe. You know Beth, and you told Madame Zoe you'd be there at two. When is Beth on time to be somewhere? Madame Zoe is a stickler for promptness, isn't she?"

Kit threw up her hands. "Okay. You've made your point. I should accept your help graciously and quit saying I can drive myself. Besides, I haven't driven with my prosthetic leg yet and that could be an adjustment. Actually I haven't driven much at all in the past years while in New York. No reason to."

Nate slanted a look at her, noting the tension he'd seen the days before in her had eased. She'd actually laughed today several times and had jumped into the planning of the fund-raiser better than he'd hoped. His goal was to give her something to do to take her mind off her problems. Sitting in the cabin dwelling on her lost leg and career would only make those problems worse. He wanted to see her driven determination back.

"You can drop me off, and I'll see if Beth or Howard can pick me up later or I can take a cab to the ranch."

"Cimarron City only has the one cab company, and you know as well as I do that they're not exactly the fastest to reply to a call. If I take you, I'm certainly going to bring you back to the ranch. I have to go into the clinic to check on a couple of animals. I'll return after that. If you're not through talking to her, I can wait. I want to show you something after that." Which was one of the reasons he suggested to Beth that he could drive Kit.

"Show me what?"

"Somehow I knew you would ask that. It's a surprise. One I think you'll like." At least he hoped she would.

"You know how much I hate surprises. I could refuse to go with you."

At the stoplight Nate shifted toward her to gauge her feelings. Kit's emotions were rarely hidden on her face. "You could, but I hope you won't. Trust me, Kit."

"Okay. Don't give me a reason not to."

"Have I ever?"

Her eyes gleamed. "No. But then we haven't been around each other in years."

"I'm going to try not to be offended by that comment." He sat forward and pressed his foot on the accelerator when the light turned green.

He was taking a risk with his plan to bring Kit to Caring Canines to meet Lexie after her visit with Madame Zoe. He knew she still wasn't convinced she should take the dog, and that she might think he was overstepping. And maybe she'd be right...but because of their past, he felt he needed to help Kit find a direction for her life. In a way, it was what she had done for him. He realized if she hadn't insisted on calling off their long-distance relationship he might never have become a veterinarian. He'd been close to dropping out of Auburn and following her wherever she went so they could be together. He hadn't wanted to play football and yet he'd felt trapped. He'd thought dropping out to be with her would be a way out of his problems. When she left him behind, he was forced to take stock of his life and decide what he truly wanted to do for himself.

By his senior year he'd found a way to fund the rest of his schooling with another scholarship and loans so that he could drop his football scholarship. He'd turned his focus to his career—as a vet, not as a pro football player, although he'd had prospects in that regard. He loved his job and hoped Kit found something to care about like he did.

When he pulled up to the dance studio, he switched off the truck and started to get out.

"I can manage by myself. Call me when you're out front again."

Nate relaxed back in his seat and watched Kit limp toward the front door. Alone. Would she continually fight any help offered?

* * *

Kathleen watched Madame Zoe's students disperse after she dismissed them, keeping back and partially hidden from view by an antique walnut wardrobe cabinet. Not far from her hung one of the photos Madame Zoe had of Kathleen. In this picture she was dressed as a firebird from the ballet by that name. She prayed no one saw her and said something. It had taken her an hour after the teens left the ranch to get up the courage to call Madame Zoe and ask if she could come talk to her. Her mentor had been thrilled, but then she didn't know the reason behind Kathleen's visit.

When the hallway cleared, Kathleen headed for the dance studio before she lost her nerve and fled. Madame Zoe had always pushed her to do better and never accepted anything but perfection. What would her mentor think of her now? She'd never put on her pointe ballet shoes again and do a pirouette—she shuddered to think of attempting one. She'd been known for her flawless pirouettes.

At the doorway Kathleen paused, took a deep fortifying breath and stepped into the room.

Madame Zoe caught sight of Kathleen in the mirror and swept around with a huge smile on her face, the warmth of it contrasting with the woman's meticulous appearance, her dark hair pulled back in a severe bun. "What a treat to see you. How long are you staying this time?"

"Awhile." She covered the distance to her mentor.

"Ah, your injury is still giving you a problem. I heard you were sitting out the rest of the season."

"What else have you heard?" Maybe Madame Zoe knew, and Kathleen wouldn't have to say the words.

"Only that you were hit by a car when the driver ran a red light, and that you'd been replaced in *Wonderland*. A friend from Tulsa had been in New York and went to see the ballet. Of course, I wasn't that surprised since your accident occurred just two weeks before that." Her former teacher tilted her head to the left and looked her up and down. "When will you be able to return to ballet?"

Kathleen coated her parched throat and said, "Never."

Madame Zoe paled, her mouth dropping open. "If it's a matter of getting back into dance shape, I'll help you with that."

Kathleen shook her head, her vision blurring. "I could do that, no matter how tough the work would be. That's not it. My leg was amputated below the knee."

"No!" Madame Zoe grasped the barre behind

her. "Not you. You had such promise." Tears welled in her mentor's eyes as she released the wooden bar and advanced to Kathleen. Her arms engulfed her in a hug. "My child, I'm so sorry. My heart breaks for you."

Why had she thought Madame Zoe would be disappointed? Her former teacher had always cared about her even when she was pushing her to do better.

When Madame Zoe pulled back and cupped Kathleen's face, the worry furrowed her mentor's forehead. "What are you going to do?"

"I don't know. That's my dilemma." *I'm not going to cry. I have to start looking for some answers.*

"I'm surprised Gordon Simms didn't say anything to me."

The conversation with the man who ran the ballet company had almost been as difficult as talking to the woman who had trained her from an early age. "I asked him not to tell anyone the extent of my injury." The dance world was a small one, and she didn't want to deal with everyone knowing. Only Gordon and a few close, trusted friends in the company knew in New York.

"So you'll be here for a while?"

"I have nothing drawing me back to New York. I sublet my apartment for a couple of months. But I'm not sure staying here is the answer, either."

"Why not for a while? I have something you could help me with. The Summer Dance Academy."

"I can't dance and my secretarial skills are nonexistent."

"But you know how to dance and teach. You did those last two years you helped me with my classes. My friend told me *Wonderland* was great, beautifully choreographed. She said you were listed as one of the choreographers. You still have a lot to offer the dance world."

"No, that life is over with." Kathleen backed away from her mentor. She'd spent the last four months telling herself that, and she wasn't going to get her hope up only to have it dashed. She couldn't be on the fringes and regret every day she wasn't out on the floor doing the ballet steps. "I can't demonstrate anything like a pirouette for the students so how am I supposed to get them to do it correctly?" It was one thing to help Carrie, but others were out of the question.

"You'll be surprised what can be done with a little ingenuity. Don't give up yet. Work for me this summer and see what you can do. Please."

"Please" was rarely spoken by Madame Zoe. She demanded from her students—nothing ever given as a request.

"I don't see how that's possible." Kathleen swung around and hurried as fast as she could from the room.

How could Madame Zoe say that to her? It was cruel to give her a glimpse of what she loved when reality would set in and end that dream.

# Chapter Six

As Nate left the Harris Animal Hospital, his cell phone rang. He quickly answered it. “Are you ready for me to pick you up, Kit?”

“Yes.”

Although Kit had only said one word, the tremble in her voice concerned him. “How did it go?” He unlocked his truck, climbed into his cab and started the engine. “Hello? Are you still there?”

“Yes. See you in a few minutes.” Then she hung up.

He’d been afraid Madame Zoe would show disappointment in Kit, and obviously by the sound of Kit’s voice, the older woman had. Maybe when she saw Lexie later, the poodle would have a good effect on her. He’d tried to help but each time she had rejected his aid. In the past Kit had always been independent, but when she had been hurting, she'd turned to him.

*Father, she needs You and the people who care about her. Help her to see that and accept she can't always do it alone.*

He turned down the street where the dance studio was located. Kit leaned against the side of the brick building. When she saw him, she hobbled to the curb and pulled herself up into the truck using the handhold. For a few seconds their gazes touched before she looked away, staring out the side window. But not before he'd glimpsed the deep sadness in her eyes. It tore at his composure.

He wanted to ask her again what had happened, but his gut instinct told him not to push, to give her time to decide what she wanted to say. She used to confide in him. Would she again? Or had too much changed between them? Were even the threads of their friendship gone?

He headed out of Cimarron City, but when he should have gone straight on the highway to reach the Soaring S Ranch, he turned left onto another road that led to Caring Canines.

"Where are you going?" she asked, still facing toward the passenger door.

"To show you my surprise."

"Oh, I forgot about that." Then she fell silent again and didn't say another word until he pulled up in front of the large kennel at Dominic Winters's ranch that housed the Caring Canines organization.

Her teeth digging into her bottom lip, she swiveled around to face him. "Why are we here? I haven't agreed to take a therapy dog."

"I wanted to show you Lexie. Emma has a couple of more days training, and then the poodle can be yours. I wanted you to meet her beforehand."

"No. No." Tears coursing down Kit's cheeks, she averted her head again.

He clenched his teeth so tightly, pain shot down his neck. He hadn't wanted to ask again, but couldn't keep from asking, "What happened with Madame Zoe?"

Her eyes shiny with sorrow, she looked at him. "I finally realized I'm never going to dance again. I think until I saw the place where I learned ballet the possibility was always there in the back of my mind, even if it wasn't logical. But now that's gone. What am I going to do?"

Emotions he'd fought so hard to keep buried demanded release. He wanted to reach out and comfort her, to pull her into his arms the way he would have once...but he resisted the urge. No, Kit would not hurt him again. He could be a friend, and if that didn't work, then he would walk away because he knew he'd never come first in her life.

"Take it one minute at a time. You're still recovering from the accident. Give yourself time to make that decision. It doesn't have to be decided right away."

"It's been four months!"

"Which is no time when you're trying to adjust to such a big change. You've barely had the time to get your prosthetic leg, make sure it fits and go through therapy to learn to deal with it. You had to have left New York right after all that was done." He'd read up on what the process involved and knew time wise she had pushed herself to be where she was, but she couldn't see how much she had accomplished.

"There was no reason to stay around."

"A big city like New York is great to visit, but I'd have a hard time getting used to living there."

"I know that." She slid a glance at him, taking in his cowboy hat, boots and jeans.

What did that look mean? She'd known even years ago he wouldn't fit in. His heart would never be there.

"Madame Zoe asked me to help her with the Summer Dance Academy after I told her about my amputated leg. I don't understand how she could do that. I can't help other dancers."

"Why not?" he asked, determined to focus on the present, not the past.

"I'm damaged. I can't dance."

"We all have things wrong with us. It's how you deal with it that's important. We can't control a lot of things in life, but we can control our attitude." He peered toward Caring Canines. "I can't force you to take Lexie, but I'm asking you to at least meet her. She may change your mind." *Because obviously I can't. I couldn't change it in the past, either.*

The door to the building opened, and Emma exited with a white poodle on a leash. She headed for the truck and rapped on the window where Kit sat.

Nate used the controls on his door to lower the passenger window. "We aren't coming in. Kit has had a long day and needs to rest."

Emma smiled. "It's nice to meet you. I'm Emma Tanner, one of the trainers for Caring Canines. Abbey's sister-in-law, Madi, heard you were coming to meet Lexie and is on her way down here to meet you. She takes ballet at Madame Zoe's dance studio and raves about you."

Nate closed his eyes for a few seconds while inhaling a deep breath and holding it. He knew it must hurt her to have to meet someone else who admired the life she used to have. He'd wanted to help Kit, but he was only making everything worse. The sound of his truck door opening filled the cab. Kit scooted around in the seat facing Emma and started to climb down.

"Stay there. Lexie is a lap dog and loves to be held." Emma handed the small poodle to Kit.

Lexie stood in Kit's lap with her front paws on her shoulders and licked Kit's face. Something changed in her expression as though for the present she was totally concentrating on the dog, remembering the one she'd had as a teen. The tension melted from her features, and Kit picked up Lexie, snuggling the pet against her.

"Except for the color, she looks just like Missy in the face." Kit peered at Nate. "She's beautiful."

"That's what I thought when I saw her. She's perfect for you."

"But Missy died. I can't go…"

"Remember, live for today. Don't worry or be concerned about the future. We don't know what God has planned for us. Missy was fourteen when she died. She lived a good, long life. And now, maybe it's time for you to let Lexie in."

Kit swung her attention to Emma. "When will she be ready?"

"I have a few more lessons I want to go

through with her. I can have her ready Tuesday afternoon. Okay?"

"Yes" came out in a hoarse whisper as Kit gave Lexie a final cuddle, then passed her back to Emma.

"I'll bring her to pick up Lexie after five Tuesday." When Kit opened her mouth, no doubt to protest, he hurriedly added, "Please, if that's all right with you. I can take you before to get what you need for her."

Kit nodded her head once, a small smile gracing her lips.

Madi, an eleven-year-old, with shoulder-length brown hair and the bluest eyes, came running toward the truck from the main house.

"I see Madi coming. Do you mind staying?" Nate asked, glimpsing a huge grin on the child's face.

"No, she isn't much older than Carrie."

"Two years ago, Madi was in a wheelchair and the doctors weren't sure if she would walk again," Emma explained. "She's one of the reasons why we have Caring Canines. She was our first client." Emma moved out of the way before Madi skidded to a halt in the opening on the passenger side.

"I can't believe I'm meeting you. Madame Zoe talks about you *all* the time," Madi said in a breathless rush.

Kit glanced at Emma, then back at the little girl. "I've heard you had a dog from Caring Canines."

"Still do. Cottonballs wanted to come, but sometimes she can cause a ruckus when she sees a squirrel. Are you getting Lexie?"

"Yes. I used to have a poodle."

"She's so sweet. She'll be a great pet for you. If you ever want to while you're here, come to the dance studio when I have class, and I'll introduce you to my friends. I have class on Tuesday and Thursday at five."

"Do you know Carrie Somers? She's my niece."

"She's in the class before mine. We go to the same school, too."

Emma put the poodle on the ground. "I'm going to work with Lexie some more this afternoon. Do you want to help me, Madi?"

"Yes. Bye, Miss Somers. Don't forget any Tuesday or Thursday. I know Madame Zoe would be thrilled." Madi stepped back and shut the door.

Kit didn't say anything until Nate pulled out onto the highway. "I'll be going to Carrie's audition next Saturday, but I don't know if I can go back to Madame Zoe's after that. I hate to let down those girls when I don't meet their expectations."

"Are you sure it's *their* expectations you're worried about or yours?"

Kit sucked in a deep breath. "You don't pull any punches."

"I never have with you, and I'm not going to start now. You're scared people will pity you and feel sorry for you, but you're doing a great job without their help."

Kit gasped. "Stop this truck."

He glanced at the anger carved into her features, her eyes diamond hard. "What are you going to do? Walk back to Soaring S?"

She pressed her lips together. "I could if I had to. This ranch isn't too far from the Soaring S."

"Two miles. And yes, you could walk back by yourself, but Howard would be furious with me if I let you, so you're stuck with me for the next few minutes."

When the wrought-iron gate with Soaring S written across it appeared, Kit broke the silence. "I don't feel sorry for myself. I feel angry. Why didn't I look to make sure all the cars were stopping before I crossed the street? All I saw was the walk button flashing. All I focused on was the fact I was going to be late for the rehearsal. The next thing I knew, I was waking up in the hospital. You're right. I can be so single-minded that I forget everything else. Checking the traffic would have taken a couple of seconds and my life would be so different. Why did God let this happen to me? He gave me the ability and love to dance and now has snatched it away."

After going through the gate to the ranch, Nate parked on the side of the gravel road, then angled toward Kit. "Has your love for dance changed?"

Her forehead knitted. "No. I wish it had, then the rest would be easier to take."

"You can still dance, just differently and maybe not on stage. Your knowledge hasn't diminished, either. Maybe you should start thinking about how you can use what you have left." He reached for her hands and cupped them between his. "God has a plan for you. Trust Him. He's in control."

"It's hard to give control over to anyone, even God."

He quirked a grin. "I know. I'm still wrestling with that. So if you stay around, you'll probably be able to throw my words up in my face." After giving her hands a gentle squeeze, Nate withdrew his and straightened behind the wheel. If he touched her too much longer, he'd find himself drawing her into his embrace and that wouldn't be good for either one of them.

At the cabin Nate walked beside Kit to the door. Part of him wanted her to invite him inside, but he knew it would be a bad idea.

On the porch Kit faced him, confusion in her expression. "Usually after a tough day, I retreat. Shut down."

"Is that working?"

Both perfectly shaped eyebrows rose. "No. I know the stages of grief, and I'm still angry at what happened to me. But I don't want to be."

"I've got a solution. Invite me in. I'll fix something for dinner and we can talk. Or not. You set the pace." Obviously he wasn't listening to the warning inside him to not get close to Kit. But then, with her he hadn't always done the logical, safe thing for him emotionally. She didn't know about the time he bought a ticket to New York to try and sway her to give them another chance to work their relationship out.

Oblivious to his thoughts, Kit said, "I know it's still early, but I'm worn out with all I've done this morning and afternoon. I don't think I could carry on any kind of conversation for long. I'm going to turn in early."

He inched closer, smelling her usual fragrance, which reminded him of sugar cookies, and took her hands between his. "Do you want me to pick up Lexie at Caring Canines on Tuesday and bring her to you or do you want to go with me?"

She chuckled. "There's a third option. I could go by myself."

He inclined his head. "True. It's your choice."

"I'd love for you to pick me up. That way I can hold her on the way home. I'll get her supplies beforehand. I know how much you love to shop and don't want to put you through the ordeal."

He smiled at her sarcasm. "You remembered."

"Like when your friend bought my birthday present? Or the time your mom got the Christmas gift you gave me?"

"Online purchasing has made my life easier." He released her hands and moved away before he thought they were both the same people they had been in the past. "Good night. I'll see you tomorrow at church."

"Maybe. I haven't decided if I'm going with my brother and his family yet."

"Then Tuesday." He stepped back and waited until Kit went into the cabin, before strolling toward his truck.

As he drove away, he wasn't sure what to think about today's events. His confused feelings swirled around in his mind until his head ached. When he arrived at his house, pent-up frustration demanded he do something physical to release it. In his spare bedroom while his Great Dane watched, he sparred with a punching bag hanging from the ceiling. But even when he finished half an hour later, he didn't have a solution to the war raging inside him over Kit.

Tuesday afternoon, bored and needing something to do, Kathleen dressed to go riding, not just in the pasture near the barn but to her special place. It was important to her to do the activities she used to when she was at the ranch. Riding to the ridge was always on the top of her list every time she came home to visit.

Behind the barn she prepared Cinnamon for their ride, then stepped up on the mounting block. With more graceful ease this time, she seated herself in the saddle, letting her left leg dangle while her right foot was in the stirrup. She was getting used to the change and so was her horse, but if she stayed, she would investigate a better prosthetic leg for riding.

She headed out and set Cinnamon in a walk. Her thoughts drifted back to the past few days. She hadn't gone to church. When her family left without her, she actually regretted the decision. At first that surprised her because she rarely attended in New York, but then Nate's words from Saturday came back and stuck in her mind.

*God has a plan for you. Trust Him. He's in control.*

She'd never been able to give that kind of control over to anyone, even the Lord, and now that she realized it, she must not trust Him like she'd always thought she did. That, too, startled her. Had she been merely going through the motions of believing, without really putting her whole heart into it?

When she reached the stony ridge, she stared up at the sixty-degree climb over rocks to the top. It was higher than she remembered and the terrain wasn't as easy to scale. But she was determined to make it to the top. She wasn't going to let the loss of her leg take away everything she loved.

After dismounting Cinnamon, she tied her to a scrub oak nearby, making sure there was shade and grass to eat. Then with her water bottle, she started up the slope—gently at first. As she planted her prosthetic leg in a pebbly patch of ground, she shifted her weight to that limb and brought her right one up, holding on to a boulder near her. Her left foot began sliding down the incline, but as she tried to adjust her balance and keep herself upright, she went down, her body slipping down the ridge.

"You're early. I thought you weren't coming to pick up Kit for another hour or so," Howard said while exiting the barn.

Nate shrugged and hopped down from his truck. "I was out this way on a call and decided to come by a little earlier rather than go into Cimarron City, then turn around and come back. A waste of gas."

Howard wiped his kerchief along his nape. "Sure, you keep telling yourself that."

"You're reading more into this than you should. I'm simply early to take Kit to pick up Lexie. Is she at the cabin?"

"Nope." Kit's brother removed his cowboy hat and tapped it against his leg, dust flying.

"Where is she?"

"You just missed her by fifteen minutes. She decided to go for a short ride."

"Which way?"

Howard pointed down the gravel road that led to the hilly part of the ranch.

Nate knew where Kit was headed. Her favorite place. "That's where the ridge is. Do you think she should climb it by herself?"

"She didn't mention she was."

"You know your sister. That's her thinking place on the ranch."

Howard sighed. "I know. But how was I supposed to stop her? I wanted to give her a little alone time. Do you really think she'll try that climb?"

In his gut he knew it. "Yes."

"I'll give her a little time, then ride out if she's not back."

"Let me ride out and check on her." Nate's stomach churned. "Now."

"You might face her wrath for disturbing her. As you said, it's her special place."

"That's okay. It won't be the first time—being there or facing her wrath."

Howard turned back into the barn. "Fine. Don't say I didn't warn you. You can take Dynamite."

Five minutes later, Nate set out in a canter toward the ridge, the whole way trying to figure out how he was going to explain his appearance. Off in the distance he zeroed in on Kit halfway up the steep hill, struggling with her footing. The sick feeling in his gut spread. He spurred Dynamite into a run.

When he arrived at the bottom where Cinnamon was tied, he quickly secured his mount to a small tree nearby, then hurried to catch up with Kit. Both feet suddenly went out from under her. Kit grabbed at a shrub as she slid on her stomach down the ridge.

It seemed as though his breathing and heartbeat stopped for a second.

As she halted her downward plunge, hanging on to a bush, he yelled, "Stay still. I'll be there to help in a few minutes." He hastened his steps, almost falling himself while he kept his eyes on Kit rather than on the ground he was covering.

She hoisted herself up toward the shrub, then sat and turned to watch him. Nate increased his speed before she could change her mind and decide to continue to the top.

"Until now I never thought how challenging this climb was," she said to him.

When he looked at her again, he noticed the dust and dirt on her front, on her face. "How many times did you fall?"

Kit lifted her chin. "Three, but I'm over halfway to the top of the ridge."

"How many times do you have to fall before giving up?"

"Never. I'm going to go up there if I have to drag myself."

The elegant set to her head reminded him of when she danced—her body moving in a graceful, fluid motion that belied the strength, discipline and determination behind it. That same determination was driving her to make it up the ridge, and he found he couldn't refuse her. If he had to carry her, she would go to the top.

When he arrived and offered her his hand, his breathing came out shallow and the beating of his heart raced. His stomach had settled, but barely.

"Out of practice, too?" She grasped it and hoisted herself to a standing position.

"Running up a hill isn't usually what I do, so yes, I'm out of practice."

She rotated carefully, using him to stabilize herself. "Why are you here?"

"I thought I would enjoy the view. It's been a long time since I've been up here."

"I can do this myself," she said, removing her hand from his upper arm and continuing her trek.

"I know and you will, but since I'm here, I hope you will let me stay."

She wobbled on her next step and quickly clutched him again. "If it hadn't been you, I'm sure Howard would have ridden out here."

With his arm around her, he assisted her upward. "Yep. See? I saved you from your brother."

"Who's going to save me from you?" Releasing her hold on him, she crested the top, a step ahead of him, and paused to take in the view.

"No one. You're stuck with me." He came over the rise and scanned the ranch stretching out below. Most of the trees had leaves on them so green they blanketed the area. "I'd forgotten how beautiful it is up here." Then he shifted toward her. "But you'll have to change before going to Caring Canines." He plucked a small twig out of her hair.

She peered at her dust-smeared jeans and T-shirt and laughed. "I can't let Howard see me."

"You can stop at your cabin and change. I'll lead Cinnamon and take care of both horses while you get dressed—again."

"Am I going to hear about this?"

"No, ma'am." He tipped the brim of his cowboy hat. "As soon as I know you can climb this without any problem. Please don't climb until you can handle it with ease."

"You're blackmailing me?"

"That's harsh. I consider myself watching out for you."

She sat on a large stone. "For your information, I'm coming up here whenever I want, and soon I will be able to climb this ridge without falling or needing any assistance. I'm not letting the loss of my leg change that."

He clapped. "Bravo. It's about time I see that fighting spirit."

She harrumphed. "Now be quiet while I mellow out."

"Don't mellow too long. We need to pick up Lexie."

She took a look at him with a twinkle in her eyes and began laughing. He would never get tired of that sound.

When Kathleen entered Caring Canines, Madi sat on the floor tossing a ball for Lexie to chase and retrieve.

The young girl grinned at Kathleen. "She loves to do this. I get tired of it before she does."

Nate came up behind Kathleen as she replied, "I appreciate the tip. Any others?"

Emma came from the back of the building in time to answer. "She hates to be brushed but loves to be scratched on her belly. Actually all over."

Madi hopped to her feet. "Cottonballs loves me to brush her. If she didn't, we'd have a problem. Her hair mats easily." She hooked Lexie's leash on, then brought her over to Kathleen.

"Thanks for the heads-up. My other poodle enjoyed being brushed." Kathleen took the leash, realizing she was making a commitment to having Lexie when she still wasn't sure if it was a good idea. What if she went back to New York? Howard had said he would take ownership if she decided to leave, but once she got attached to the dog, Kathleen knew she probably wouldn't want to say goodbye, which would mean taking Lexie with her. Pets were common in the city, but it was more time-consuming to take care of them there because they would have to be walked. And still in the back of her mind she didn't know if she should take on another commitment with her life so up in the air.

Lexie rubbed against Kathleen's right leg. She bent over and scooped the poodle up into her arms. The dog felt right cuddled against her chest.

"Thanks, Emma," Nate said next to Kathleen.

She peered at the trainer. "Yes, I appreciate you taking the time. I…" Tears filled her eyes, and she swiped at her cheeks while hugging Lexie to her. "I'll do my best," she said in a shaky whisper, then pivoted and hurried toward the door, wet tracks running unabated down her face.

# *Chapter Seven*

Out in the warm spring evening with not a cloud in the sky, Kathleen halted at Nate's truck and lifted Lexie to snuggle against her cheek. "I cry so easily these days. This isn't me, girl." The poodle licked a tear from her face, her tongue tickling Kathleen. She chuckled. "You do know how to cheer someone up."

"Is something wrong?" Nate's deep voice sounded behind Kathleen.

She swept around. "No. Yes. I guess it has to be if I'm crying. I've been doing that a lot lately. So not like me. My emotions have swung from one extreme to another ever since I returned to Cimarron City. They say you can't go home."

"True only in the sense it will never be like it was. Everything changes over time. But there is still plenty to return to."

"Should I go back inside and say something to Emma and Madi?"

"No, I told them you were happy about Lexie."

"If I tell you I am, you're going to be so smug your plan worked that your head is going to swell, and you won't be able to wear your cowboy hat."

"I'll get a bigger size." He took Lexie from her arms so she could climb into the cab, and then he gave her the poodle. "Emma told me she eats in the morning so you don't have to worry about it tonight."

When Nate rounded the Silverado and sat behind the steering wheel, Kathleen said, "Beth and I went shopping this morning for supplies for Lexie. I also got some more groceries. I didn't want to always have to go up to the house to eat. How about staying for a supper? Nothing fancy."

"Sounds nice." He slanted a look at her. "You clean up good after that dust bath you took on the ridge."

She shrugged. "What's a little dirt when I'm proving a point?"

"What point?"

"There may be changes in my life, but I refuse to allow everything to change. I'm more comfortable in the saddle now that I've been riding every day. I'm not giving up my favorite place on the ranch. You've got to admit it's beautiful up there." Kathleen stroked Lexie lying in her lap, the action calming, soothing a restlessness in her.

"I see the lure."

"The past few days has shown me I need to see about getting another prosthetic leg. The one I have is for living in New York City and walking around there. I've been researching about riding and other more active exercises with a prosthetic leg. There's a different model that's a better option, although I've adapted for what I have. I want to be able to make it to the top of the ridge." Today halfway up the hill she'd realized she had to prove something to herself. "By myself."

"You'll be able to. In the short time you've been back at home I've already seen changes. Your fighting spirit is coming back in full force." Nate drove through the Soaring S gate. "Maybe coming to the ranch has broken the cycle you were in."

"Maybe." Had it started when she'd told Nate, then her niece and nephew about her amputated leg? Maybe that had helped her truly grasp what her life was now. But understanding the truth—even accepting it—didn't make it any easier to live with it. Especially when she still wasn't sure what she wanted to do with her life.

"Keeping busy will help you. You've always been so active. It can't be easy having to take it slow recovering from the accident and surgery." Nate pulled up to the cabin and switched off the engine.

"That's what I've been thinking lately. I'm going to see Madame Zoe at the auditions for the academy. If she still wants me to help, even if it isn't teaching a class, I think I will, especially if Carrie gets in." Was there really a chance that she could stay in the dance world, in a small way? She hoped so, but she couldn't be sure. Not yet.

"And if she doesn't?"

As Kathleen opened the passenger door, she smiled back at him. "She's good for her age. I'm going to think positive and help her in the evenings this week."

Inside the cabin Kathleen cradled Lexie next to her cheek. "This is your new home. Later I'll show you some of the ranch."

She put the poodle on the floor, and Lexie began sniffing around the living room, then made her way into the kitchen and finally the back of the house.

Nate stood behind Kathleen, his hands on her

shoulders, kneading the tension that knotted her muscles. "She's going to love it here."

As Nate's fingers worked the stress from her, the sight of Lexie trotting back into the living room and making a beeline for her gave her a sense of calm and peace she hadn't had in a long while—even before the accident. She didn't let herself wonder why.

"That turkey-and-Swiss sandwich sure hit the spot." Nate finished off his iced tea, then stood and grabbed their plates to take to the sink.

"You must be easy to please. There wasn't much to it. Slap a few ingredients between two pieces of bread." Kit followed him into the kitchen off the living area.

Nate started to rinse the dishes, but Kit clasped his arm to still his movements. Her touch zipped through him, reminding him of what they used to have.

She tugged him away from the sink. "You're my guest. What kind of hostess would I be if I let you clean up?"

"A smart one."

Her eyes gleaming, she pulled him toward the living room. "I think I'm being insulted."

"In that case, I'm not saying another word. I want you to invite me back for dinner."

"Do you cook for yourself?" Kit gently shoved

him down onto the couch and then took the other end of the sofa.

"Yes. Sometimes I experiment with gourmet recipes. Sometimes they work, sometimes not."

She chuckled. "I don't do fancy at all. I was hardly at my apartment in New York between performances, rehearsals and dance classes. That's why as I'm getting my energy back, I'm going crazy doing nothing. Riding once a day and having an occasional cooking lesson from Beth aren't enough." Lexie hopped onto the couch and settled down next to Kit, who laid her hand on the poodle and absently scratched her behind the ears.

"Speaking of something to do. I'd like the entertainment committee to get together Saturday morning at the church at nine. I can change it to another time if that interferes with the auditions."

"No, actually that will work. The auditions start at one. I've been thinking of a couple of things we could do. But I want to talk to Howard first to see if it's possible."

"Possible? What are you thinking about doing?"

"The perfect place to have this shindig is the old barn. We could make changes, even put up a stage for the Western show, and it won't interfere with the running of the ranch. For the show,

I was imagining something that could showcase the teens' talents. For instance some of them could do a couple of scenes from *Oklahoma.*"

"Remember when you played the lead in high school?" Watching her perform had emphasized to Nate how important it was for Kit to pursue her career on stage. Until then he'd never realized how emotionally expressive she was with her body.

"That's what gave me the idea. The last act can perform the song 'Oklahoma' and I can choreograph a dance. It's our state song so it seems appropriate."

*Our* state song. As though she identified with this place. There was a time he didn't think she did. All she wanted was to leave and seek her career, especially in New York. "We'll talk about it on Saturday. I can pick you up and make sure you get to the auditions afterward."

"That would be great. Beth and Howard are going to the auditions so I can catch a ride home with them. But that reminds me, if I'm staying at least through summer, I'm going to have to work out transportation. My brother doesn't know it, but he's going to loan me his automatic pickup while he uses the standard one."

"Maybe I should warn him."

Kit nudged him in the arm with her elbow. "If he knows about it beforehand, I'll know who leaked the info. Besides, I'm not 100 percent sure I'll be asking him. It depends on how long I end up staying. I'm not sure yet what I'm going to do so I'm not going to do anything right away. That seems to be the story of my life lately."

He wasn't going to let her go down the "poor me" path if he could prevent it. He pushed off the couch and held out his hand for her to take. "Let's walk Lexie and introduce her to the Soaring S."

The poodle perked up when her name was mentioned, and she stood up on the cushion.

"I'll get her leash. I hope after she gets familiar with the area she won't have to use one while we're here at the ranch." Kit allowed him to draw her to her feet, only inches separating them.

His heartbeat kicked up a notch. His gaze fixed on her lips, and all he could think about was kissing her. He moved away before he acted on that thought. That would take them in a direction they shouldn't go. Kit needed to figure out what she wanted. He did, too.

After Kit secured the leash on Lexie, Nate held the door open and waited for them to go out onto the porch. When he came up beside Kit on the sidewalk that led to the gravel road, the darkness of evening shadowed her expression. The night surrounded them, the breeze light and warm. The scent of animals nearby drifted to Nate, mixing with the honeysuckle and roses along the front of the house that perfumed the spring air. Stars littered the black sky and a sliver of the moon reflected little light for them to use on their trek.

"I'll get a flashlight out of the truck in case we need it." Nate hurried and retrieved it from the glove compartment, then jogged back to her side.

"I'd like to walk away from the main house and barn. We can investigate where I think the shindig should be." Kit waved her arm toward the ranch's gravel road that dead-ended at an older barn used for storage.

While Kit held the leash with one hand, Nate took her other one. In the darkness, even with the flashlight illuminating their immediate path, he didn't want her to stumble. That was the only reason he clasped her hand.

*Yeah, right.* He'd missed this closeness with a woman. After he and Kit broke up, he'd thrown himself into the college scene, even dated and became engaged. But he and Rebecca had both realized he'd been on the rebound and it wouldn't work for them. That was when he threw himself into his studies, quit football and finished college early.

At that point, everything had revolved around

getting his degree and starting a practice. So he guessed that Kit and he weren't so different after all. He loved his work and didn't know how he would handle it if he lost a chance to be a vet. When he thought of it that way, he could partially put himself in Kit's shoes and realize how difficult this adjustment was for her. He would support her, but if he fell for her, he was only setting himself up to be hurt again.

Nate arrived at the church with Kit early Saturday for the scheduled meeting with the other members of the entertainment committee. There were five teens, Kit and him. As he suspected, Steven had come early, too.

"I need to talk to Steven. It won't take long," Nate said in a low voice close to Kit's ear.

"Fine. There's Debra and Anna. I'll keep them company. I want to see if Anna is ready today for the audition."

As Nate strode toward Steven, the teen moved farther away from the kids coming into the rec room until he ended up in the corner with nowhere else to go.

Nate studied Steven's face—the edgy mannerisms from biting his fingernails to the jitters. "I can tell something is wrong. What happened?"

"Dad and me..." Steven sucked in a deep

breath "…we had the biggest fight. Ever. I left. My friend said I can stay with him. I can't go back home."

"What did you fight about?"

"What do you think? What we've fought about this whole last year. I finally did something about it. Yesterday, I told my coach I wouldn't play football next year. Dad got a call from Coach this morning. I know you probably don't understand, but I hate the game my father loves."

Nate felt transported back seven years ago when he had said the same thing to his own father. But the argument had taken a different direction then. Nate's father had seen football as a means to an end—paying the way for Nate's future. They just didn't have the same view of his future. In the end Nate was able to finish college without the football scholarship, which had gone a long way to mend fences between him and his father. "I've been in your shoes, Steven."

"When you played football for Cimarron High School?"

"No, I was on board with playing football in high school, not because I loved the game—although I did—but because it was my way to college. But there came a time it began to stand in my way of what I wanted to do for my future.

My dad didn't understand how I could walk away from a free-ride scholarship."

"You did that?"

Nate nodded. "I couldn't devote enough time and energy to my studies, and they were suffering. I wanted to get into veterinary school and that meant my grades had to be really good, not just passing." Like Kit he couldn't give his classes the focus he needed to do well because so much time had been spent involved with football. At the time Kit broke up with him, he hadn't understood that when she'd told him. Now he did. "It wasn't an easy decision, but it was the right thing to do. Eventually my dad began to see my view."

"I don't think mine will ever understand."

"Give him time and talk to him again."

Steven's frown carved deep lines in his forehead. "I told him we could enjoy the game together as spectators, but he was still mad at me."

"He still needs time to adjust to the change. A lot of people react negatively to change." Kit popped into his thoughts. She was in that place now. He prayed time would help her adjust to her new life.

"My dad and me have always been close. But lately…" Steven snapped his mouth shut, a nerve twitching in his jawline.

"My dad and I were close, too. Still are. My

decision didn't end that. Are you going to stay at your friend's tonight?"

"Yeah. Mom thought it would be a good idea, and she will try and talk to Dad while I'm gone."

"Sounds like a good plan." Nate glanced over his shoulder at the other members of the committee seated and waiting on them to start. "If you need me, I'm there for you. Are you ready to meet with the others or do you need some time?"

"I'm okay. Maybe this'll help me not think about my problem."

As they started for the group, Nate clapped Steven on the back. "Time is a great healer."

Time was what allowed Nate to be comfortable helping Kit now. Right after their breakup, his emotions would have been too raw, and he wouldn't have been able to be around her as he was now. She needed him to be a friend, and that was exactly what he would be. Just a friend. Nothing more.

"I think the planning meeting went pretty well. What do you think?" Kathleen asked as she settled into the front passenger seat in Nate's truck later Saturday morning.

"Too smoothly. The kids loved everything we talked about. The show. The square dancing contest. They agreed to everything. Teens don't do that. Also we have a good game plan for how to use the time we have left before the fund-raiser. We may actually be able to pull it off." He drove away from the church. "Should I be worried?"

"My only experience with kids comes from my niece and nephew, and they aren't teens yet. Still, I don't see any reason why we should be concerned. They're a good group of kids. And if something goes wrong, we'll deal with it. Most of the people attending the Western Shindig will be from the church. They'll understand if there are a few problems." She relaxed back and surveyed the area. "We're going the wrong way. Shouldn't we get something to eat near the high school where the auditions will be held?"

"I have to meet Abbey Winters at the animal hospital. One of the dogs at Caring Canines hurt his leg. Her dad is out of town for a long weekend, so I'm on call if there's an emergency."

"So that was the call you received at the end of the meeting. I'm glad Dr. Harris is getting some time off. I don't know how he ran his practice without your help."

"I won't be surprised if he takes on another vet in the next year or so." Nate parked at the side of the animal hospital. "This shouldn't be too long. Abbey and Emma pour a lot of time into the dogs they train. I want to make sure the dog is okay."

Kathleen smiled and thought about this morning waking up with Lexie sprawled out next to her on her bed. When Kathleen moved, the poodle was instantly up and greeted her with a wagging tail. It had immediately lifted her spirits, along with the thought that she had a busy day ahead, which always gave her something to look forward to. She'd missed that since the accident.

"I haven't told you—" she glanced away "—but Lexie was the right call for me." When she returned her look to his face, appreciation marked her expression. "Thank you for thinking of it. I wouldn't have, and it's great having her there at the cabin with me." Kathleen exited the pickup.

Nate met her at the front of the Silverado to walk in the side door. "I love my Great Dane, although sometimes he can get a bit overzealous when he greets me. Usually when I've been gone a long time."

"This will be Lexie's first test of how she deals with separation. The past three days she's been by my side. She even went riding with me yesterday—or rather she ran beside Cinnamon and me."

"To the ridge?" He moved inside behind her so she didn't see his expression.

But she could hear the concern in his voice. She peered over her shoulder at him. "Yes. But to make you feel better, I didn't go up to the top. I'm waiting for my new prosthetic leg, which is geared for that type of activity. On Thursday I went to be fit for one."

"Good." Relief eased the anxious look on his face.

Madi stood in the hallway to the exam rooms with Abbey. The little girl saw him and hurried toward him, frowning, her eyes shiny. "Dr. Nate, Spanky got out of his fenced area when I opened the door. I chased him, and when he jumped over the stream out back, he didn't make it across. His front leg hit a stone. He's been whimpering and limping. I tried to catch him before he got outside."

Nate laid his hand on Madi's shoulder. "I know you tried. It's not your fault. He's high-spirited and obviously needs more training."

Abbey stepped forward, extending her hand to Kathleen. "I'm Abbey Winters, Madi's sister-in-law. You must be Kathleen Somers. Madi talked and talked about you Tuesday night. She's excited you're going to be watching the auditions."

"I'll be cheering her and my niece on."

"Where's Spanky?" Nate asked as he passed them in the hallway.

"Exam room two. I'll come with you and hold him while you check him over." Abbey glanced back at Madi. "Why don't you sit in the reception area and keep Miss Somers company?"

As Nate and Abbey entered the second door on the right, Madi led Kathleen to the empty reception area. Kathleen took a chair, but the child paced, twisting her hands together.

"Dr. Nate will fix up Spanky." Kathleen hoped to calm the tension pouring off the girl.

She stopped and faced Kathleen. "I know he will. He's the best, but I'm scared Abbey will decide not to keep training Spanky. He'll do great one moment, then suddenly do whatever he wants. A service and therapy dog has to be obedient, and he's flunking that."

"Not all dogs are cut out to be service or therapy dogs."

"I know." Madi's shoulders slumped. "He was a stray. He won't have a home."

"Maybe you could find him one. Do you have a friend who wants a dog? Ask around at school."

Madi's expression brightened. "I might." A smile splashed across her face. "I was so worried because I don't think Abbey and Dominic would let me take in another animal."

"You take in strays?"

"When I can. I'm the one who found Spanky and talked Abbey into training him." Madi began pacing again, glancing at the clock over the reception desk.

"You'll make it to the audition in time. You have an hour before you have to be there."

"That's not what I'm worried about."

The child's face showed every emotion she felt. It reminded Kathleen of herself at that age. As she became an adult, she'd learned to hide what she was feeling most of the time—except when she danced. Then she let everything flow from her heart.

"Madi, what's the problem?"

"I'm trying to remember my dance. I can't. I don't think..." The girl's voice faded. She scrunched her forehead, her eyes narrowed as though in deep thought.

"Do you have your ballet slippers with you?"

"In the car."

"Go get them and put them on."

"Why?"

"Every time I've thought I've forgotten my dance it all came back to me when I put my pointe shoes on. See if that'll work for you." Kathleen could remember how panicky she would get right before a big performance. Giving Madi something to do rather than worrying about her audition would hopefully help her.

Madi raced from the reception area and was back in a couple of minutes with her shoes in hand. She plopped into a chair and quickly donned her ballet slippers.

"Now why don't you show me your dance? I'd love to get a preview."

Madi's eyes bugged out. "Really?"

"I can give you some pointers if you want."

"You'll teach me?" Madi grinned widely.

Kathleen nodded. "Imagine the music you're dancing to is playing and start whenever you're ready. Be sure your arms follow through each move you make."

A faraway look appeared on Madi's face, and suddenly she began. After a final pirouette, she ended with her right foot pointed on the floor in front of her and her arms curved softly above her head.

Kathleen clapped. "Bravo. Nice work, especially extending your arms when you needed to."

Madi beamed.

When Abbey and Nate came into the reception area, Madi whirled around. "I did my dance for her. Kathleen Somers. I can't believe it—she liked it."

The first time Kathleen had had her dancing

complimented by a world-renowned prima ballerina in New York, she'd had that same excitement and smile on her face. She was humbled by Madi. Kathleen wasn't anywhere near the level of the prima ballerina. Watching the child demonstrate some of her steps for Abbey and Nate, this time with no hesitation, made Kathleen revisit the idea of helping Madame Zoe as a dance instructor. She'd been contemplating it since she talked with Nate on Tuesday, but now she realized she needed to give it a try at the very least.

Abbey looked over Madi's head and mouthed the words, "Thank you."

"How's Spanky?" Madi asked Nate finally.

"He'll be okay after a couple of days of rest. He didn't break his leg, but it's badly bruised. He's going to stay here until you all can come back and pick him up."

"We'd better leave now." Abbey turned toward the hallway. When Madi started to follow her sister-in-law, Abbey added, "Aren't you going to change into your tennis shoes?"

The girl threw a grin over her shoulder toward Kathleen. "Nope. As long as I have them on, I won't be nervous. I'll be careful where I walk outside."

As the pair left out the side door, Nate stood in the doorway, his gaze fastened on Kathleen.

Her cheeks began to heat from the intensity in his look.

"You told her your trick," Nate said in a husky voice. "You're going to help Madame Zoe, aren't you? Teach a dance class?"

Her blush deepened. "Yes. Seeing Madi brought back memories of when I was her age. Madame Zoe once invited a retired dancer friend to visit our class. This woman was in her late fifties and used a cane when she walked, but when she was young she'd danced all over the world in some big ballet companies. At eleven I knew who she was and seeing her was so exciting. When she taught our class one time, she didn't perform the steps, but I learned a lot that day she worked with us. I might be able to do the same for others."

He held out his hand for her, and she took it. "Let's go. We can use a drive-through for lunch since I figure you'll want to get to the audition earlier than planned."

A warm fuzzy feeling suffused her at his touch. At the side door, he sent her a look that heightened her awareness of him: the pine scent of his aftershave, the curl of his hair on his nape, the sandpaper roughness of his fingers, the gleam in his eyes that drew her in as though they were connected.

*Maybe there's still something between us. Maybe—*

As he ordered their lunch, she reined in her thoughts. She couldn't think of a future with anyone now. Too much was up in the air for her.

In the lobby of the high school, Nate stood near where Kit sat, resting her leg after the long day she'd had. He hadn't planned on staying for the auditions, but he'd enjoyed the time spent with Kit and didn't want it to end.

Kit glanced up at him, exhaustion evident in her expression. "You don't have to stay to wait for the list to be posted. I'd planned to get a ride home with my brother."

"I know, but since I was here for Anna, Carrie and Madi's auditions, I want to know if they got in."

Kit shifted her attention to her niece, who stood between Beth and Howard, leaning against a wall not far from where the list would be posted. "She's worried. She chews her lip when she's nervous."

"So do you."

"Maybe it's a family trait," Kit said with a laugh.

"How did she do?"

"She did fine, but Madame Zoe only takes a couple of kids under ten."

"How are Madi's chances? Anna's?"

"Madi's are a little better because she's eleven and I can't imagine Anna not getting in. She's very good."

"What year did you start the summer academy the first time?"

"Eight."

"Why am I not surprised?" Nate's gaze captured Kit's, and he winked. "Madame Zoe knew you had potential from the beginning."

"And Carrie knows that. I'm afraid of how she'll feel if she isn't picked."

"She has you to help her." Nate tossed his head toward the auditorium door that just opened. "The waiting is over."

"Good. Because the waiting is the worst part."

"Even if Carrie doesn't make it?"

"Yes." Kit pushed to her feet and moved toward the board where the list would be posted.

Nate hung back. Some cheers erupted. A couple of girls started crying. Anna strolled away from the board with a big smile on her face. Good, at least she made it. He'd known how important ballet was for Anna. She talked about it all the time—like Kit used to do.

Nate rubbed his hand across the back of his neck. There were some fathers here, but the group in the lobby was mostly made up of women and young girls. Why had he stayed? What did he think he was going to accomplish? Had he really stayed just to spend more time with Kit? That was a dangerous thought. Kit had made it clear there was no place for a relationship in her life right now and he had to agree.

She talked about New York as though she was only here visiting, and the fact she still had her apartment only reinforced she hadn't let go of her life there. If there was a way for her to participate in the world of ballet in New York, she would take it. He knew that in his heart, especially after seeing her at the audition, helping the girls before it started. And that meant she'd leave him again.

Madi made her way to the front of the line to view the list. She looked at it and began jumping and yelling, "I made it."

Not far behind Madi, Carrie pushed forward in the crowd around the board, Beth right behind her. Carrie whirled about and buried her face against her mother. The child's shoulders shook.

He covered the distance to Kit. "She didn't make it."

Kit frowned. "Not this year."

Carrie tore away from her mother and ran

from the lobby, shoving open the double doors to the school and heading outside. Beth started after her.

"Beth," Kit called out. "Let me talk with her. Okay?"

Beth nodded. Kit limped toward the double doors and disappeared outside. But she came back inside a few minutes later and hastened to her sister-in-law and brother.

"I can't find Carrie."

## *Chapter Eight*

Fear swamped Kathleen. "I looked in the parking lot and all around the area. Carrie's gone."

Her eyes wide and tear-filled, Beth frantically glanced back and forth from Kathleen to Howard to Nate, who joined them. "I tried to prepare her for the possibility she wouldn't make it. But all she said was that you got in the first year you could."

"Let's go outside and spread out." Nate started for the double doors.

Kathleen, Beth and Howard quickly followed.

"She'll be all right. She's probably hiding somewhere because she's upset." Kathleen prayed that was all. *God, please don't let anything happen to Carrie.*

In the parking lot, Nate gestured toward the west side. "I'll take this area."

"I'll go in the opposite direction," Howard said and began searching to the east.

"Let's check around the building," Kathleen suggested. "I remember there are some great hiding places by the bushes. I'll go left. You right, Beth. Okay?"

Her sister-in-law stared across the four-lane road that ran in front of the high school. "What if she went that way? There are a couple of fast-food restaurant across the street. She may be hungry. She wouldn't eat lunch because she was so nervous. You saw her stumble at the beginning of her dance."

"Do you want me to help you check those places first?"

Beth shook her head. "You go around the school building. I'll go across the street." She pointed toward the middle restaurant. "She loves chicken nuggets from there."

"Did she have money?"

"No, but she might not realize that until she's there. She was so upset when she stormed out."

"Then go." Kathleen hastened to circle the school and begin searching.

As she neared an alcove sheltered by bushes that Kathleen remembered on the side of the building, she couldn't shake the feeling she was responsible for Carrie's reaction. She should have prepared her for the very real possibility that Madame Zoe wouldn't choose her this year. She rarely selected a child eight or nine. All those years ago, Kathleen had been the sole exception.

Once she'd asked Madame Zoe why she allowed young girls to try out. She'd told Kathleen she was always looking for another child like Kathleen. While that flattered her, she saw the harm in that. It hadn't bothered her in the past because she knew how tough the ballet world was and believed that girls needed to be prepared for that. Then she witnessed Carrie running from the school in tears. Had she become so toughened she forgot that side of dance? The disappointment. The heartbreak.

She peered around the scrub and spied Carrie sitting on the ground with her legs pulled up to her chest and clasped. She quickly texted her brother that she'd found Carrie. "Honey, let's talk."

"I'm no good." Sobs infused Carrie's voice.

"Yes, you are." Kathleen squeezed through the narrow opening between the bush and wall and sat with some difficulty next to her niece. She slid her arm around Carrie who immediately turned toward her and cuddled against her, hiding her face in Kathleen's shoulder. "You're not even nine yet."

"I will be tomorrow."

Kathleen could barely hear her niece's muffled words. "You haven't been dancing long. Madame Zoe has only taken a few eight-and nine-year-olds."

"You were one of them."

"Yes, but I started dancing at five. I took a lot of classes. I knew then I wanted to be a ballerina."

"I want to be one. Just like you."

Kathleen's heart ached. "It takes so much work. I had to give up a lot to do what I did."

Carrie lifted her head, her eyes glistening. "I can do that."

"You don't have to make that decision right now. You're still young. Give yourself time to be a child." She'd given up a lot of her childhood because she'd been so certain that dancing was what she would do with her life, and in one instant all her hard work had been destroyed.

Carrie's bottom lip stuck out. "I guess I don't have a choice. Madame Zoe didn't want me." A whimper invaded her last sentence, and she sniffed.

"I want you."

"But you're my aunt."

"I can help you with your dancing this summer. It'll be fun, us working together."

Carrie knuckled an eye. "I thought you were helping Madame Zoe."

"I will some, but you're more important to me."

"Where? This week we worked outside on the deck, but we can't do that all summer. It'll get really hot soon."

"I can come up with somewhere. My living room would work. Think about it. Talk to your mom and dad. You can let me know."

"Carrie. Carrie."

The sound of Nate's voice reminded Kathleen that other people were searching for her niece. "We need to let everyone know you're okay."

Carrie rose.

Kathleen started to stand and realized in the small confined area with little to help her she would have trouble getting to her feet.

"What's wrong, Aunt Kit?"

"I haven't mastered getting up from the ground yet."

"I'll help."

"Tell you what. Go let Nate know you're okay and that I texted your dad to let him know I found you."

"I'll get him to come help."

"No. You don't need to. With more room in the alcove, I'll be able to manage."

Carrie's eyebrows knitted. "Sure?"

"Yes." Sort of. At the very least, she was sure she needed to try on her own. People wouldn't always be around to help her.

Once Carrie disappeared, Kathleen rolled onto her right side and put both hands on the ground. She pushed herself to a kneeling position, then using her good leg and clasping the brick edge of the alcove, she rose slowly. Leaning a little into the wall, she paused to get her balance before making her way out to the side of the school.

As she emerged from the hedge, the first thing she saw was Nate rushing toward her. She held up her hand and said, "I'm okay," then leaned over and brushed some dead leaves from her jeans.

He slowed his gait, but now Kathleen noticed her brother and Carrie hurrying across the grass toward her. Embarrassment warmed Kathleen's cheeks. She didn't want to be a burden or concern for anyone. She wasn't helpless. Didn't they understand that?

"What did Carrie tell you?" she asked when Nate arrived a little out of breath.

"That you were on the ground and couldn't get up. I thought you'd fallen."

Ten seconds later her brother and niece came to a halt in front of her. "Carrie Somers, you shouldn't have worried them like that. I wasn't hurt or in any danger, and I didn't want any help. I just needed a little time and room to get up by myself." Kathleen shifted to Howard.

"I've had to relearn a few things. I can't just pop up like I used to. At least not right now. But that doesn't mean I can't stand on my own."

"Sorry, Kit. I guess we all overreacted, but I'd rather do that than leave you somewhere hurt." Howard pulled out his cell and called Beth to let her know Carrie was safe and with them.

"I don't know about you all, but I'm ready to go home." The active day was finally catching up with Kathleen. "Ready, Howard?"

Howard blushed. "I brought my truck. I forgot that you'd be riding back to the ranch with us. Nate, will you bring my sister home?"

Nate pushed up the front of his cowboy hat, laughter dancing in his eyes. "Yes, but it isn't like you to forget something like that."

"You try getting two females ready on time and out the door. I thought we were gonna be late for the audition."

Kathleen folded her arms over her chest. "Sure. Now that I think about it, I believe you're up to something."

"Dad thought Dr. Nate could bring you home and maybe stay for dinner like he did the other night."

Howard snorted. "I didn't say that."

"No, Mom told me."

Beth arrived. "I heard my name. I told you

what? Not to run off like you did and scare your family silly?"

"About Dad playing matchmaker."

Howard's red face deepened in color. "C'mon. I have a few chores at the ranch." Howard stomped off with Beth and Carrie trailing at a much slower pace, holding a whispered conference.

A few yards away Carrie turned and backpedaled. "Dr. Nate, I'm having a family birthday party tomorrow evening. You're invited. Aunt Kit will give you the details." The child didn't wait, but whirled around and quickened her step.

"They all are conspiring together," Nate said with a laugh.

"I'm sorry about that. I don't know what my brother, Beth or my niece think they're doing. I'll set them straight."

Nate tugged his hat down in place. "So will I. Well, at least Howard. How about we get some dinner on the way to the ranch since we didn't have a proper lunch earlier? I know how much you can eat. What little we had before the auditions isn't enough to keep you going, is it?"

"That's changed, too. When I was exercising and dancing eight or ten hours a day, I burned a lot of calories. Not anymore. And I was told to stay within about eight pounds of my current weight or I'll have to get a new prosthetic leg."

"Really," Nate said as he strolled toward his truck, "I guess I can see that. Will that be hard?"

"Yes. I love food and have always been able to eat whatever I wanted because I knew I'd burn it off. Now I can't." Just another consequence of her accident she had to deal with. Since getting out of the hospital, she had put on five pounds. "In fact, I need to lose some weight. I want to keep on top of it."

"Let's go to Carlos's Mexican Restaurant. You used to love it, especially the salads, and the food is still delicious."

"I'm glad something is the same. But I can't stay long. My exhaustion is catching up with me."

At his Silverado Nate opened the passenger door and took her arm.

She looked at his hand on her. "I'm tired, but I can still get into your truck by myself."

He grinned, a dimple appearing in his cheek. "Sorry. My mama taught me to open doors for ladies. It's a nasty habit that's hard to break. I'll try harder not to next time." He winked at her and sauntered around the front of his pickup, whistling the title song from *Oklahoma*.

When he sat behind the steering wheel, she asked, "Are you making fun of me?"

"I've lost my touch if you can't tell." He started the engine and pulled out of the parking space.

Kit let Nate into her brother's house Sunday evening. Her greeting smile instantly lifted his spirits—exactly what he needed after counseling Steven again today. The teen and his father still weren't talking. Nate could see it at church earlier, sparking his own memories of the few weeks after he'd quit college football.

"I hope Carrie likes my present." Nate held up a hot-pink bag with bright-colored polka-dotted tissue paper.

"What is it?" Kit tried to peek inside.

He pulled the gift away. "You'll just have to wait and see."

"You sure know how to torture a gal."

"It's not your birthday, but I seem to remember you have one in July." He rubbed his chin. "Hmm. I'm going to have to think hard on what I want to get you. I remember how important birthdays are in your family."

Kit swung around and strolled toward the back of the house, slanting a look over her shoulder. "Not to me anymore. My birthday is just another day." She winked and disappeared into the den.

He laughed. He liked this playful side of Kit.

He hadn't seen it in a long while. The more she became involved in her career the more serious she'd become. But the girl he'd fallen in love with all those years ago had loved to laugh.

When he entered the room, he came to a halt a few feet inside. Obviously the rest of the Somers didn't agree with Kit that birthdays were to be low-key. Dozens of multicolored streamers hung from the ceiling. A large banner hanging from the mantel proclaimed Carrie turned nine today. A long table in front of the fireplace held a feast. The centerpiece was a cake decorated in white frosting with hot pink, lime-green and turquoise glittery stripes across it. In the middle a ballerina wearing pointe shoes with her arms curved above her head drew everyone's attention.

When he saw the ballerina, he searched out Carrie to see how she was doing after the auditions yesterday. A huge grin plastered her face as she talked with her mother and Kit.

Howard came up to Nate. "I'm glad you could make it."

"So I can give you another opportunity to fix me up with Kit?"

"Yes. You would be good for her. You were years ago."

"Sorry. That didn't work out. I'm not a young man anymore who thinks all you have to do is love someone and everything will work out."

"But you're here. It must mean you still care."

Nate turned toward Howard. "I'll always care, but that isn't the same thing as being in love and marrying someone."

"If you say so," Kit's brother murmured and moved into the center of the room to get everyone's attention. "It's time for Carrie to open her presents because this guy here—" he pointed at himself "—is starved and wants to eat, especially the cake Beth made."

Everyone jockeyed for a seat on two couches facing each other. The gifts were stacked on the coffee table between the sofas. Nate waited for the family to sit, then eased down next to Kit, the only place left.

Beth handed her daughter Nate's bag first. He was amazed at the child's restraint as she first opened the card, then carefully pulled out the tissue paper until she found the rectangular box at the bottom.

Nate leaned toward Kit and whispered, "You certainly haven't rubbed off on your niece. You used to tear into your presents. There were times I thought you might destroy what I got you in your haste."

"I've mellowed since then."

Carrie opened the box and lifted out a delicate silver chain with a cross on it. She smiled at Nate. "Thank you. It's beautiful."

And from her expression, Nate knew she really meant it. Her smile, however, shifted into pure glee as she put down the necklace and grabbed up the next present. With each gift after his she ripped the paper off it and threw it over her shoulder behind the couch. She dove into the presents as though she was starved and a banquet was set before her.

Kit murmured into his ear, her breath tickling him, "Beth told her she had to be polite and take her time with your present. This is her usual behavior. At Christmas she beats the whole family in getting her gifts opened first. A gal after my own heart."

"All's well with the world. It has been righted again."

Kit playfully punched him in the arm. "I do believe you are making fun of me, or is it the Somers family enthusiasm you're mocking?"

"Neither. It's nice to see that not everything changes over time."

Kit chuckled, her attention swinging back to Carrie as she reached for the last gift.

It had to be Kit's because everyone else's was strewn in a chaotic mess about Carrie.

The girl paused and eyed the big envelope, then peered at Kit. Their gazes locked and Carrie carefully worked the flap up and pulled out the card. Tickets fell onto the child's lap. Her eyes lit up as she picked them up. "Season tickets to the Tulsa Ballet Company." Awe caused her voice to slowly build to the last word. Carrie shot up and rushed around to Kit. "Thank you! This is the perfect gift. I hope you'll go with me this fall."

"I will, if I'm here."

The corners of Carrie's mouth drooped. "I thought you were staying. You're helping Madame Zoe this summer."

"I'm staying for a while, mostly because I want to help *you* this summer."

Kit's words hurt Nate. He knew she needed to reassure Carrie, but again he felt he came in second in her life. It was a tough pill to swallow, even though it shouldn't have been. They weren't a couple and Carrie was family.

The girl's smile returned. "Is it possible a couple of my friends could be part of the lessons? One tried out and didn't get it. The other two wouldn't even try out for the dance academy because they thought they didn't have a chance. This would make their summer if you would let me."

"If I'd wanted to refuse I couldn't after that plea. Sure. Let's start our first class this next Saturday first thing in the morning, and then when school lets out the following week and I have my schedule from Madame Zoe, we'll figure out when to meet. But I want you to remember I might not be here the whole summer."

Nate tensed at the repeated reminder that she might not stay.

Carrie held up two fingers. "Twice a week?"

"Are your friends serious about ballet?"

Carrie nodded.

"Then we'll try three times a week if that's okay with their parents."

Carrie jumped up and down. "That's the best present ever. I'm gonna go call them right now." The child raced out of the den before Beth could react.

"I guess it's okay if we dig in. But—" Beth looked pointedly at her husband, who had moved a couple of steps toward the food table "—the birthday cake is off-limits until Carrie returns."

Howard threw up his hands. "I know."

Seeing the playful teasing made Nate yearn for a family. He'd always thought he would marry and have children but after two attempts, he wasn't sure if he was meant to be a husband.

He stood and offered Kit his hand. Without hesitation, she clasped his and let him pull her to her feet. "Are you sick?"

Her forehead scrunched. "No, why do you ask?"

One corner of his mouth tilted up. "You let

me help you up without a word about how you don't need my assistance."

She moved into his personal space, her proximity causing his pulse to speed. "It's been a long day with church, then riding with Carrie and Jacob. It was nice to have help—this time."

"Let me know, then, when it's okay to offer," he said with a laugh.

She inched forward. He inched backward. "I know that I've been extra sensitive about trying to do things myself. I'm trying to learn to accept help graciously. It's not easy. I've always been so independent."

"I know." Nate stepped back again several feet, drawing Kit toward him. He didn't want the whole family listening.

"Then I'm asking you to have patience as I swallow my pride and accept assistance when I need it."

The beseeching look she sent him melted his heart. If everyone weren't trying to stare at them, he'd be tempted to kiss her. He pressed his lips together and nodded his head once, his gaze fastened on her. The pull toward her was strong. He dragged his attention away and looked over her shoulder. All four family members quickly busied themselves with loading their plates with food.

"Before we become the entertainment for your family, we'd better get our dinner."

A soft blush colored her cheeks.

As she crossed to the table, Nate hung back for a moment, regrouping his scattered emotions. It didn't take much for Kit to pull him back into her life and that scared him. Just ten minutes ago, she'd warned the group she might not be staying in Cimarron City.

Kathleen opened the door to her cabin, scooped up Lexie waiting in the entrance, then entered with Nate coming in right after her. Something had changed tonight at Carrie's birthday party. When she placed her hand in his, something deep inside her shifted as though until that moment she hadn't given herself permission to ask others to help her. She didn't have anything to prove to her family or Nate.

Nestling her dog against her, she started for the back of her place. "I want your opinion about fixing up the other bedroom as a dance studio. It's much larger than my bedroom and with the furniture out of the room, I think it'll work."

Inside her grandparents' bedroom, she held Lexie in the crook of her left arm and swept her other across her body as if performing a ballet step. "What do you think? I'll have floor to ceiling mirrors down this wall." She pointed to the one that was long and uninterrupted by a door or window. "There would be a barre there and another one on the opposite side between the two windows."

Counting off footsteps, Nate maneuvered around the bed and went from one end to the other. "It's about twenty feet by fifteen. Is that big enough?"

"It is for small groups or—" She bit back the words she almost said.

"Or what? You can't tease me with half the sentence." He closed the space between them.

"Or if I want to dance for myself. Everyone tells me, you included, that I can still dance. I want to see if I can."

Nate swallowed hard. "Just so you realize it won't be the same."

"I know that. But Madame Zoe wants me to choreograph a dance for the students at the Summer Dance Academy to perform at the end. I don't want to run through it at her studio. I need my own space, especially with Carrie and her friends taking lessons this summer from me."

"If it meets your needs, go for it. Does this mean you're thinking of staying longer?"

"I'm not committing past the middle of July when the dance academy is over with. Honestly

I don't know what I'm doing from one day to the next, but as I become more proficient with my prosthetic leg and my strength and energy return, I have to do something with my time. I don't like what I was becoming when left with nothing to do." Why was she going to all this trouble if she wasn't going to use it past the middle of July? She might teach after July, but if she didn't, at least she would have a private place to dance for herself.

"I can help, if you need it. It's going to require some work."

"Great. I was hoping you would volunteer. I want to keep the cost down by doing as much as I can myself. I'll have to hire someone to put the mirrors and barres up. But I want to refinish the wooden floor and paint the room a bright color."

"Who is going to remove the furniture?"

"Howard and the ranch hands. There's a storage shed for old furniture he'll store it in."

"So you have it all figured out. You've been busy."

Kathleen tried to stifle a yawn but couldn't. "I was up most of the night. I couldn't sleep until I came up with a solution for where I would have Carrie's class. I thought first about the living room, but that's a more radical change to the cabin. I think Granny would be pleased with what I have planned for her bedroom."

Nate took Lexie from her and put the dog on the floor, then clasped Kit's upper arms and tugged her to him. "I think you're right. She was one of your biggest cheerleaders when you performed."

"One?"

"I was the other."

"You were?" With the way dance had come between them, she was surprised he'd say that.

"You make your body tell a story. I used to find myself caught up in your movements."

Tears welled in her eyes. "You never told me that."

"I was a teenage boy. I didn't know how to say it out loud without sounding like an idiot."

She lifted her hands and cradled his face. "Thanks for telling me now. I always thought you tolerated my ballet like I tolerated your football."

"Hey, you didn't think my body told a story when I caught a ball and went for a touchdown?"

She laughed. "I'll admit you were beautiful to watch on the field when you ran."

He looped his arms around her. "When you get your new leg for exercising, maybe you can run with me."

She embraced him. "We'll talk about that at a later date."

"Oh, that's right. You were never a big fan of running."

"I might change. Certainly other things have."

He should let her go, but her beautiful face mesmerized him. For the life of him he couldn't step away from her. He bent his head toward her, his lips brushing across hers.

# *Chapter Nine*

Kathleen should have pulled away from Nate's kiss, but she was frozen, unable to move other than closer to him. His arms tightened around her as if he never wanted to let her go. She relished the moment of being cherished. It had been so long. She felt whole, and for a few seconds she forgot that her life was totally topsy-turvy. Pouring her suppressed emotions into the mating of their lips, she clung to him, her heartbeat racing, her breathing shallow.

When he parted, he laid his forehead against her, his hands cupping her face. "Don't ever doubt how special you are."

A little voice in the back of her mind wanted to shout, *No, I'm not. What do I have to offer?* But she squashed those doubts for the moment. She wasn't going to let them ruin a nice evening with Nate. Almost like old times—except they weren't the same people they had been back then.

That thought finally sobered her, and she disengaged, putting some space between them.

He stared at her for a tension-filled moment, his body taut, his arms stiff at his sides. "I know I shouldn't have kissed you, but I don't regret it, Kit. We've shared a lot over the years and I can't forget that. I tried to and obviously I haven't been very successful."

*Me, too.* But she wasn't going to admit it to him. How could she, when she was floundering, trying desperately to hold on to part of her old life?

"I didn't regret the kiss, either. I've been going down memory lane a lot since I returned home. The auditions for the Summer Dance Academy yesterday were definitely a journey I took for years," she continued, purposefully turning the conversation in a new direction. "However, Carrie's experience made me see them in a different light."

"Because she didn't make it?"

"Partly. But today I couldn't stop thinking about the girls who want to learn to dance but don't plan to pursue dancing professionally, especially as they get older. So often people have the mindset that if you participate for a long time, then you want to turn it into a career. Not everything in life is a competition."

"Sadly for many, it is."

"I want Carrie to love ballet for the pure enjoyment and beauty of the art form."

"She isn't the only one struggling with enjoying something just because you like it. That was what was bothering Steven yesterday. He enjoys football, but not on the level for competition. He wants to experience it for fun or as a spectator. His father doesn't see it that way."

"I'm worried about how Anna sees ballet from some of her comments before the committee meeting started. She's good, but you have to be more than that to make it in the ballet world. We'll see. I'll be teaching her level for the summer." Kathleen looked away, staring at the dark night out the window. A long sigh escaped her. "I know what it's like to get close to your dream and have it snatched away as you reach out for it." She brought her gaze back to Nate. "But I had nothing to fall back on. I wasn't prepared for that option. I thought I had years before I couldn't perform anymore."

"Life can change instantly." Nate snapped his fingers. "That's why we can't worry about the future. Wasted energy."

"Easy to say. Hard to do."

"I know." He smiled and walked toward the

door, pausing for a second next to her and giving her a light kiss on the cheek. "Let me know when I can help you with getting the studio ready."

"I will." She grasped the edge of the door as he left, watching him disappear into the darkness.

The feel of his lips lightly touching her cheek stayed with her as she turned out the lights and headed for her bedroom.

On the following Saturday after her first class with Carrie earlier, Kathleen dipped her roller into the soft-pink paint in the pan, then started on the second wall in her new studio. "It's official—the kids are out of school for the summer. You should have seen them celebrating yesterday."

"I remember those times. Ah, to be young again." Nate began at the opposite end from Kathleen. "We should get through today, then refinish the hardwood floor tomorrow. When is your next class with the teens dancing for the fund-raiser?"

"Wednesday. That should give the floor time to dry and hopefully give me enough time to teach them the dances before the shindig." She glanced toward him, seeing her reflection in the mirrored wall next to Nate. She looked a sight with splotches of pink all over her and stray strands of hair hanging loose from the bun on top of her head.

His gaze snagged hers, a twinkle in his gray eyes. "Yes. You look fine."

"Who said I was concerned?"

"Your pinched mouth."

"Okay. I'm not a very good painter. There's more on me than on the walls. How do you manage not to get any on you?"

"I'm motivated. Pink wouldn't be a color I would wear."

"It's a good thing this morning I taped off the windows, doors and mirror. It took some time, but if I hadn't, people would have thought I'd given Jacob and his friend the paint and brushes, then left them unsupervised."

"You'll wash up nicely." He gestured toward the walk-in closet. "You took the door off. Why?"

"It's going to be my office. I know it's small, but mostly I'll store the music and recorder in there."

One of his eyebrows hiked up. "Office. This is sounding official, long-term."

Kathleen shook her head. "No, but it will be more of a time commitment than I'd realized. Carrie found many other kids that aren't doing the dance academy that would like to have a lesson once or twice a week, and I can't fit them all into one class session. I'll also have a class in the afternoon on Tuesday and Thursday for them until the middle of July when the dance academy ends. I'm not committing any longer than that."

"That's longer than you said three weeks ago when you arrived. What changed your mind?" Nate finished one section and sidestepped to start on a new section of the wall.

She lifted a shoulder in a shrug. "I don't want to move on without any idea where I'll go or what I'll do. This seemed as good a place as any to stop and regroup."

"Have you heard from anyone in New York?"

"A couple of friends have texted me what's going on."

"How do you feel about that?"

"They're good friends, and I want to celebrate their successes with them, even the woman who took my place in *Wonderland.* At first it was hard to see her and not think about what I can't do." Kathleen painted the same area several times before she realized it and sidled toward Nate.

"And now?"

"I've started thinking about how she's bringing to life the steps I put together for one of the dances. It's become easier to handle."

For the next ten minutes they worked in silence. She chanced a look toward Nate and glimpsed a thoughtful expression on his face. What was he thinking about? She hadn't seen much of him during the past week, but he'd called her a couple of times—mostly to talk about fund-raiser plans.

Tomorrow after church the youth group would come out to the ranch to start working on the old barn. With only three weeks to go, he'd always start out their conversations talking about that, but before they hung up they always ended up talking about their day, something they used to do when they'd dated. Falling into that pattern seemed so natural and a bit disconcerting. She decided the quiet took her thoughts in a direction she didn't want to go—thinking about the future. She was trying to take it one day at a time and felt she could cope when she did that.

"After we finish the third wall, do you want to go riding with me? With my new prosthesis, I can lock my knee in position, and I bought boots with a heel, which will help. That way I can keep my left foot in the stirrup."

"So that works for you?"

"I tried it out the other day. I did much better. It feels more natural to me, and Cinnamon is becoming quite accustomed to the changes."

"Have you gone back to the ridge yet?"

"Yes, a couple of times. I only tried once again to climb it."

"How far did you get?"

She stretched her arm as high as she could to reach the top of the prepared wall with her roller. She was glad that Nate painted the area close to the ceiling before they started. "I went a third of the way up before I fell. My other leg has the bruises to prove it. Instead of trying to go on like that first day, I stopped, rested and then made my way down the slope. That took all my energy."

"Did Howard or Beth go with you?"

"No, they weren't around to tell." Kathleen kept her attention on the patch of wall she was painting, but she didn't have to look at Nate to see the frown—the concern on his face.

"That's not smart to go on your own. I know you're used to doing everything by yourself, but what would happen if you fell and broke your right leg, with no one there to get help?" Disapproval dripped off his voice.

Her teeth dug into her lower lip. She wanted to protest, but she knew he was right. "I hadn't intended to climb, but I've been doing better and thought it would work. I guess that was wishful thinking."

"Tell you what. When you have the urge to tackle the ridge again, call me. Let me climb it with you, then when you can do it without any help, have at it. If you want to try today, we can."

"After painting this room? Probably not a good time, but how about Memorial Day? You aren't working, are you?"

"Nope. My turn to have the whole day off. Dr. Harris is covering any emergencies that come up."

"Then how about early morning?"

"How early?"

"Come for breakfast at eight, and then we'll go to the ridge." When he didn't say anything, she shifted toward him.

His stare drilled into her for a long moment. "What made you change your mind about doing it alone?"

"You. I see the ridge as a goal for me to complete. In dance I always set goals for myself to accomplish, but when I needed help with a technique or a dance step, I would seek someone to help me. This really isn't any different. But the bottom line was the thought of breaking my good leg and probably being confined to a wheelchair for a while. I'm used to aches and pain when I'm working to achieve something, but letting my pride get in the way of safety isn't smart."

A slow smile curved his mouth, his eyes tender and caressing. "I'll be here at eight, Monday."

Nate stood next to Kit at the bottom of the hill, staring up at the top of the ridge. The bright sun warmed his back. A light breeze carried the scent of the cattle herd in a nearby pasture and rustled the leaves on the cottonwood tree near a stream, sending the white cottony seeds flying.

Nate passed the walking stick to Kit. "This should help keep you stable. I've done my share of hiking in the Smoky Mountains, and it has come in handy."

"Thanks. Since I didn't get many chances to hike in New York other than the subway stairs and concrete streets, I never thought of this." Kit inhaled a huge breath as though fortifying herself for the task before her.

"I'll be near to help when you need it. Otherwise you'll do what you can by yourself. Will that work for you?"

She threw him a grin as she set out for the base of the hill. "Yes."

Kit scaled the lower fourth without any difficulty but the next section was riddled with small rocks and pebbles and the incline was steeper. "This is where I run into problems."

Nate pointed up twenty yards. "See that level part? Make it there, and we'll rest. Then you can decide if you want to go further today. Nobody said you had to do it all in one day."

Kit stuck her walking stick in the ground above her and planted her right foot near it, digging the stick in for stability. Nate stayed behind her, watching to make sure she remained steady and upright, especially when she moved her prosthetic leg. Slowly, one step at a time, she ascended the rocky incline, glancing back every once and a while at him. Sweat coated her face, and she had to periodically wipe her hands on her jeans to avoid losing her grip on the walking stick. When she arrived at the more leveled terrain sixty feet off the ground, she stopped and waited for Nate to join her.

He came up beside her and clasped her upper arms. "You're doing great. I think the key is going slow."

She raised her gaze to the top. "Before I used to scramble up it in ten minutes. It took me twice that time to make a third of the hill. Sometimes I think it might as well be a mountain."

"A mountain-hill you're going to conquer." His look seized hers.

For a few seconds doubt shadowed her eyes, but then she gave her head a shake and said, "Yes. I'm feeling better each time I ride Cinnamon. Each time I climb, I'll go a little farther until I stand on top again and shout to the world I made it by myself."

"So you aren't going to count the time I helped you?"

"Not the same thing. For months I've let my determination waver in this battle. Not anymore."

"Good. Now, do you want to go farther or come back another day?" He released his hold on her, although all he wanted to do was draw her into his embrace and kiss her again. Maybe he would when they made it to the top.

"Let's go further. See that place up there? I want to try and climb to it."

Nate noted another level spot about fifteen feet above them. "I'm right behind you."

Kit kept up her pace, but as she neared her goal, her right foot began slipping as she moved her left one. Nate started to grab her, but she clutched a lone scrub close by, stopping her fall. She paused, catching her breath, then continued the last few steps. When she reached her goal, she dug her walking stick into the loose ground and swung around to wait for him.

"I did it. Now, if only that scrub would follow me up the hill."

He chuckled. "Quick thinking but I wouldn't have let you fall."

"I know."

Her tone and expression nearly undid him. She hadn't given him that look in years, and for the first time in a long while, he wondered if there was a chance for them after all. He couldn't take his eyes off her.

Before he forgot they needed to return by eleven to help, as Howard said, "the second day of the barn raising," Nate dragged his attention away from Kit. "We'd probably better head back. The kids and their parents will be here in forty-five minutes, and I don't want you to take the fast way down."

"Like in the nursery rhyme when Jill tumbled down the hill after Jack?"

"Yep. We need to go slow and easy like we did coming up."

She chuckled. "I love that you're including you in the 'we.'"

"Personally I ought to leave Howard to get everything started. He's the one who roped me into doing this. He's the one who invited everyone back today."

"Probably because he's starting to panic. We have a lot to do to get the barn ready for the hoedown." Kit started to descend.

"Wait. This time I'll go ahead of you, and I hope you mentioning Jack and Jill doesn't mean anything."

Thirty minutes later, Nate gave Kit a leg up onto Cinnamon, and then he mounted Dynamite.

"Let's walk the horses back to the barn and give my brother time to have everything organized. I'll need to stop by the cabin and get Lexie. I promised her she could go if she behaves."

"In a short time you've wrapped that dog around your little finger."

"No, it's the other way around. Thank you again for thinking of getting me a dog."

"You're welcome, Kit."

Side by side they rode together across the pasture, toward the newer black barn in the distance. A thoughtful expression descended on her face. At times like this he wished he knew what she was thinking. The morning had gone well, so why the pensive look?

That question nagged him all the way back, and while Kit went to her cabin to get Lexie, he strolled toward the old barn, realizing he was ten minutes late and everyone had arrived except Steven. As Nate dove into the work that needed to be done, he glimpsed Steven getting out of an SUV, slamming the door hard and storming toward the barn. Daniel Case parked the car and climbed from it, glaring at his son.

Nate walked toward Steven's dad. "Are you going to be able to stay and help?"

The man evened out his angry expression and peered at Nate. "I was going to, but…" He sought his son out in the group of teens inside the large double doors to the barn. "I don't know if it's a good idea."

"Is there a problem? Maybe I can help. Steven's been a big help. He's volunteered to paint the stage backdrop. What I've seen so far is great."

Daniel Case snorted. "That's the problem."

"Doing the backdrop?"

"He told me on the way over here that he's taking art next year. He'll have an extra hour because he quit football and his mother signed his class schedule right before school was out, okaying the change." A nerve in his jaw jerked. "He prefers drawing over football. What has gotten into him? I know he talks to you. I know you used to play ball. Why haven't you talked some sense into him? I can't, and my wife supports Steven."

"I understand Steven doesn't like playing football. In high school I had a friend like him. When his heart wasn't in the game, he got careless and was injured. He ended up out the whole season with a torn rotator cuff. Sad that his father tried to get the doctor to let him play with it that way," Nate couldn't resist adding.

The glare directed at Steven drilled into Nate.

"Have you been filling my son with this nonsense? Is this why he feels that way? Football is good for him. It teaches him sportsmanship and how to be part of a team."

Nate waved his arm toward the barn and the kids Steven was working with. "It seems to me he's learning that right now. In fact, he's in charge of the scenery and displaying good leadership qualities."

Daniel's face turned red. He opened and closed his mouth. "Tell Steven I'll come back and pick him up in three hours."

"I hope you'll reconsider staying."

The man swung around and tramped back to his SUV. While he pulled out, gravel went flying, his tires screeching.

# *Chapter Ten*

As Kathleen stepped out of the cabin with Lexie trotting next to her, she couldn't get the morning out of her mind. No, she hadn't reached the top of the ridge, but so much had happened. She had gone farther than any other time all by herself without falling to the ground. Was it because Nate was behind her as a safety net? She was getting so used to him being around. She was becoming dependent on him. Thinking about him first thing in the morning and the last at night.

Then when he said her name—Kit, the one she grew up with—it felt right. She wasn't Kathleen Somers anymore. That name was associated with her ballet career and New York.

The noise of a car speeding from the old barn area warned her right before it barreled around the bend in the road, heading toward her and

Lexie. Afraid her dog would run out in front of it rather than move to the side with her, Kathleen—no, Kit—quickly bent over and scooped Lexie up into her arms, but the sudden action caused her to lose her balance. She fell, rolling into the small ditch nearby.

Stunned, she checked Lexie for injuries. The poodle barked and licked her. Reassured, she struggled to sit up, hugging Lexie against her as she tried to get her bearings. The driver of the SUV slammed on his brakes, coming to a stop a few yards down the road. While she closed her eyes and composed herself, the sound of a door closing came to her. She wished the man would leave. With her nerves jiggling, she didn't want to deal with him.

"Are you okay?"

*Go away. Please.* Her left side took most of the impact when she hit the ground. Now it was beginning to throb.

"Ma'am, should I get you some help?"

She opened her eyes and stared up at the middle-aged man wearing a look of concern as he squatted near her.

Lexie growled.

"Shh, girl. It's all right," Kit finally said, rubbing her cheek against her dog, then lifting her gaze to the stranger, probably a parent of one of the teens helping with the shindig. "This is a working ranch with children. No one drives over twenty miles an hour on this road." To his credit, the man looked properly abashed. She put Lexie on the ground next to her. "Stay."

Her dog sat, waiting.

"Here, let me help you up." The man stood and held his hand out.

Not sure what to do, Kit just stared at him. She didn't want to struggle to get up with a stranger, especially since she didn't know if she'd hurt her left leg. What if it didn't work right?

"Are you sure you're okay?"

She started to reply when she heard Nate say, "Kit, what happened?" as he raced toward her.

"I fell, but I'm fine."

When Nate stopped next to her, he turned his attention to the driver. "Did something happen? The way you drove away from the barn was reckless. Are you the reason she fell?" Nate's hands curled and uncurled by his side.

The man dropped his head. "I was angry and…"

"And what? Not thinking?" Nate kept his tone and expression even, the only sign of his state of mind was his fists at his sides.

"I wasn't." The man shifted his gaze to Kit. "I'm sorry. Please let me help you up."

She exchanged a look with Nate, hoping he

picked up on her need to do it herself or at the least without a stranger looking.

"I'll take care of Kit. I think you should leave, but don't forget to pick up Steven. Football isn't worth this anger between the two of you. No game is."

Steven's dad mumbled his apology again and trudged toward his SUV. When he drove away, he kept his car at an appropriate speed.

Nate knelt and waited until the SUV disappeared from view before saying, "May I help you up?"

Kit felt her prosthesis through the jean material. "I think my leg is okay." She rolled over on her hands and knees, then used Nate to help pull herself to a standing position with her good leg taking most of her weight. Then she tested her left one and took a couple of steps, relieved that nothing worse than some scrapes and aches protested the movement. "I'll be okay. The more I move around the better I'll be. Falling easily, especially at first, isn't uncommon."

"How did it happen? Did you have to jump out of the way of the car?" A hard edge sharpened Nate's voice.

"Not exactly. I wanted to step off the road because he was driving hazardously for the ranch, but when I grabbed Lexie to get her out of the road, it threw my balance off and I went down."

He pressed her against him. "I'm just glad you're all right, but if you have problems, please see the doctor. I know how you are about going to a doctor, but—"

"I will. I'm better about that than I used to be. For a while those were the only people I saw."

"Do you want to go back to the cabin? The kids will understand."

"Nope. I told Steven I would work with him on the scenery with what I had in mind for the show." She glanced toward the road. "I'm assuming that was Steven's dad. Why was he so mad?"

"Steven is quitting football and his mother supports him. She agreed for Steven to take art instead of football next year. I think Daniel just found out, and he and Steven had words on the trip to the ranch."

"Steven does good work. I'm impressed with the barn mural he's doing for the backdrop. He has talent."

"Tell that to his dad. On second thought, don't. It would probably get him all riled up again. We don't want any more accidents."

"My body totally agrees with you. I've always been used to moving quickly, and I can't do exactly what I used to do. I have to accommodate for my leg."

*Thank You for sending Nate to assist my less-than-graceful rise from the ground.*

While Lexie walked beside Kit, Nate clasped her hand and started for the old barn. As she neared the teens, she tried not to limp more than she usually did, but she couldn't help favoring her left leg. The kids knew she had been in an accident, but she'd never told them she'd lost her leg. She'd never found a way to make that announcement or fit it into a conversation.

Inside the barn, she slipped her hand from Nate's but almost immediately wanted to snatch his back. Suddenly she felt as though she was going in front of an audience for the first time. Her stomach churned and beads of sweat popped out on her forehead.

*That's ridiculous. No one saw what happened.* And yet she couldn't rid herself of the butterflies fluttering through her nervous system, threatening to take over.

Lexie stood on her hind legs, her front paws pressing into Kit in a gentle reminder that her dog was there for her. Bending over to pick up Lexie, she moved too quickly, making her head spin. She swayed but managed to lift her poodle into her arms while Nate stepped closer.

Anna approached her. "Are you okay?"

Kit imagined the war of nerves visually battling on her face, especially as the adrenaline caused by the near collision with the SUV had subsided, leaving her shaking and freezing in the seventy-five-degree temperature. Kit clung to Lexie. No words of reply came to mind.

Nate slid his arm around Kit's shoulders. "She fell. Just shaken up a bit."

As one dancer to another, Anna let her gaze skim down Kit's length. "Is that why you're limping more? Maybe you should see a doctor in case you injured your leg. Is it your ankle?" Anna pointed toward Kit's left one.

Kit's eyes grew round, and she backed away. "No!" The one word came out more forceful than intended.

Anna's mouth formed a big O, and tears instantly sprang into the girl's eyes from the harsh tone. "I didn't mean..."

In that instant Kit realized she couldn't keep the extent of her accident quiet. She couldn't hide behind long pants and act like everything was the same. It wasn't. Anna would be in her class at the Summer Dance Academy as well as rehearsing for the fund-raiser at the ranch. She should be aware of Kit's situation.

She stepped away from the shelter Nate offered, raised her chin and squared her shoulders while still holding Lexie for support. If she told Anna, then the rest of the teens would know quickly. "My left ankle isn't hurt, because

I lost that leg from the knee down when a truck hit me in January. I've been dealing with getting used to a prosthetic leg for the past three months. My fall just now brought all that back as well as the fact I landed on that side when I went down."

As Kit spoke, Anna's gaze dropped to Kit's leg then back up. The girl started to speak but no words came out. More tears welled into her eyes as she finally said, "I'm sorry. I'm so sorry."

The kids nearby stopped what they were doing and listened to their conversation, but Kit didn't care who knew anymore. Hiding it didn't make it any less real. And right now, Anna was upset. Kit didn't want that.

She moved to the girl and pulled her into a hug. "It's okay. I'm dealing with it."

"But you're never gonna dance again. You're never gonna be on…"

"The one thing I learned over the years is to never say 'never.' All things are possible through the Lord."

"But not that." Anna pulled back, wet streaks running down her face. "I've wanted to be like you ever since I started at Madame Zoe's."

Those words were bittersweet to Kit, but she would never let Anna know. "I'm honored and you can still strive for what I did. One day I'd love to be in the audience watching you dance your first principal role."

Anna smiled through her tears. "I'd love that."

Kit looked around and leaned close to Anna. "I think we have an audience."

Sniffling, the teen wiped her hands across her eyes. "My first role will be dedicated to you."

"With that kind of thinking, you'll make it." Kit had seen Anna dance and knew she had the ability to become a lead ballerina. "Because talent is only part of what makes a star. Drive and determination are very important."

Kit's heart expanded as she looked at Anna and remembered how she had been at that age. Eager, hopeful, willing to do the work necessary. Had it been worth it? Yes, but her life was different now, and not accepting that fact would only make her journey forward more difficult.

"Are you going to work on the scenery with Steven and me?" Kit asked Anna, aware no one in the barn was doing anything but watching them.

"Yes. I'd been sent to find you. Steven needs your advice about how to do the last scene with the song 'Oklahoma.'"

"Tell him I'll be right there."

As Anna moved away and everyone set to work again, Kit turned toward Nate. "I've learned you can't hide from the truth. It always comes out, usually when you don't plan for it. This wasn't what I envisioned for today."

"Are you okay?"

When she looked into his eyes, the lump in her throat melted. "Yes. I actually feel like a weight has been lifted and now is the time to move forward. For that, I thank you."

"I didn't do anything."

"You did more than you realize. You didn't give up when all I wanted to do was wallow in self-pity. Neither did my family. That's probably why I came here. In my heart, I knew they wouldn't give up on me and that was what I needed. Now the big questions is what do I do with the rest of my life."

"You don't have to decide everything in one day. You have time."

Kit spied Steven coming out from behind the backdrop and moving toward her. "No, but I'd better help Steven. Something must be wrong. He's frowning."

Kit parted from Nate and walked to Steven. "Anna said you needed me to help you with the scenery."

"Did my dad have anything to do with your accident earlier?"

"Why do you ask that?"

"Because I saw him tear out of here and then

you show up shortly after that, limping from a fall. Anna told me what you said."

"Yes, but everything is fine now. The more I walk the better it is. Once I take off my prosthetic leg and adjust it, I should be okay." Although the group now knew of her prosthesis, she didn't want to make an adjustment in full view of everyone. "Let's go back behind the stage, and while I'm fixing my leg, you can tell me about your problem with the scenery."

For a few seconds Steven stayed still, staring out the entrance. Finally he joined her. "I don't understand my dad. Why is football so important to him? I can't believe what he did today."

"Did you ever ask him why?" Kit took a seat on a step to the stage. "Did he ever play?"

"Yeah, in high school, but he never talks much about it."

"Ask him." Kit rolled up her wide-legged jeans. "Now, what do you have in mind for the final scene?"

As the sun beat down on Nate later that afternoon, he removed his cowboy hat and used it to fan his hot face. "At least we got the painting finished. Now, let's hope the rain holds off until it dries."

Howard came down from the ladder leaning against the old barn and stepped back to take in the newly painted exterior. "Beth wanted us to make it red. I had to put my foot down and insisted on black. She thought red would add character to the place and my sister agreed with her."

"I can see Kit wanting red over black. That was always her favorite color."

"You see what I'm up against," Howard said in mock horror while his eyes gleamed. "Two women. Three if you count Carrie."

Nate chuckled. "And you love every minute of it."

A grin lifted one corner of Howard's mouth. "I'm glad Kit came home. She's been here not quite a month and I see the old Kit peeking out." He tapped his finger against his jaw. "I wonder if a certain vet had anything to do with that."

"Don't go there. I've seen your little maneuvers to get us alone. We're friends. Our relationship now is different than when we were teens."

Howard's thick eyebrows rose. "I would hope so. I want this one to last."

Nate huffed. "I'm leaving before you have us married in that delusional mind of yours." He caught sight of Daniel parking his SUV and walking toward the entrance. "I've got someone I need to speak with."

Howard grasped his arm. "I'm coming with you. I have a few choice words to say to that man for what he did earlier."

"Let me handle it."

Kit's brother stared at him for a long moment, then nodded.

Nate headed inside, hoping to stop Daniel before he talked with Steven, but he was too late. Steven met his dad halfway, anger hardening his features. Steven planted himself in front of his father. The teen's body stiffened as his eyes narrowed on Daniel.

"I heard what you did when you left. What were you thinking earlier? You could have killed Kit. She has nothing to do with what's between us." Intensity swirled around Steven.

From where Nate stood, it was easy to see that the teen was bigger and more muscular than his father.

"I know. I was wrong."

"Did you know she was in an accident in New York in January? Hit by a car running a red light. Did you know that she lost part of her leg and has a prosthetic one?"

The color drained from Daniel's face. "No… there's no excuse…" The man glanced around at all the teens and parents watching the exchange. "We'll talk at home" finally came out of his mouth, but the words were weak, almost sounding defeated.

Nate approached the pair. "Let's take this outside." He spied Kit coming out from behind the backdrop, Lexie right beside her. Kit homed in on Steven and his dad. Nate hurriedly ushered the pair out the back of the barn, away from the teens and adults helping.

Daniel pivoted toward Nate, peering beyond him. Nate knew Kit was coming up behind him. When Daniel strode toward her, Nate waved Steven back to keep him from interfering. He'd seen regret on the man's face.

Daniel stopped in front of Kit. "Please accept my apology. I never meant you any harm. All I've been doing for the past couple of hours is driving around, trying to sort stuff out. Are you sure you're okay? I was foolish and reckless. Please forgive my behavior."

A smile graced Kit's face, lighting up her features. "Of course I forgive you. But will you do me a favor?"

"Anything."

"You should be careful promising that," she said with a teasing note in her voice. Then her expression sobered. "Please talk to your son. Really talk to him."

As Steven closed the few feet between Daniel and Kit, Nate intercepted Steven before he broke in. Nate moved the teen away a couple of yards. "Anger won't get the answers you need. When you talk with your father, you want him to listen and hear you. He'll want the same thing. If Kit can forgive him for his reckless driving, then you need to also. We never know what tomorrow holds. Don't regret today."

Steven inclined his head.

"Son, we'd better get moving. Your mom has an early supper planned." Daniel waited for Steven, and then the two walked through the barn and out the front.

Kit watched them leave. Nate came up behind her and laid his hands on her tense shoulders, then began kneading them.

She sighed. "I needed that after the day it's been."

"Your revelation was the talk all through the barn. The ones who didn't overhear you talking to Anna heard it from her. Her admiration for you has only grown." Nate turned Kit to him. The red patches on her cheeks didn't surprise him. He caressed the back of his hand across her face, feeling the warmth against his skin. "You never did like the fame part that went with your job, but you need to realize how much she looks up to you. Anna couldn't believe how calm you were in accepting what happened to you."

"I guess that was one of my better performances because there has been nothing calm about my reaction to my circumstances. Still, I'm beginning to see fighting it is only harming me." She lifted her gaze to his, tenderness in her eyes that stirred up all the feelings he'd once had for her. "Home has a way of doing that to me. That's why I came back when it wasn't working out in New York. I couldn't get past the anger. But I hadn't planned to say anything to the kids today."

"What made you?"

"It felt right. I knew that Anna would tell the others and everyone would know by the end of today. That's why I didn't say to her not to say anything about my prosthetic leg. I can't run away from my problem anymore." She tilted her head to the side. "What did you say to Steven at the end?"

"I suggested if you could forgive his father, Steven could forgive him, too. I hope those two will talk it out tonight."

"So do I."

He wanted to kiss her, to feel her in his embrace, to forget everything that had happened between them years ago that had sent them their separate ways. He looked long and hard into those expressive blue eyes and felt lost as he had been as a teen. *I can't go there.* He backed away a couple of steps, their gazes still bound. His throat burned. He moistened it, but still suppressed emotions jammed it.

*I can't fall in love again.* The memory of the pain flooded him. He dragged his attention to the stage area. With most of the workers gone, the sound of the big fans filled the quiet. The air around him was cool in the shade.

"You, Steven and your crew did a great job. When are you going to start rehearsal with the dancers and singers together?"

"Next week, which won't give us much time. Thankfully the production will only be part of the entertainment or I would be panicking."

"You're a pro. It will work out."

In the center of the barn Kit slowly rotated, scanning the beginning stages of the transformation. "This will be a nice place for the party and a good use for the space. When my dad built the new barn closer to the main house, my grandpa wasn't happy. He told him there was nothing wrong with this one and I have to agree. I think Dad just wanted everything more convenient to his house. My grandparents built and lived in the cabin, which is closer to here. I think that was the only time I saw my father and grandfather have an argument."

"It was so sad when your dad died from a heart attack. So young, but Howard did a great job taking over the ranch right after his high school graduation."

"Dad had been working with him for years."

Nate grabbed at the chance to talk about her parents and grandparents. Anything that would take his mind off the dilemma he faced as his feelings for Kit continued to grow. He learned from his mistakes. He didn't repeat them, and yet he could see that in Kit's case, he was in real danger of getting his heart broken again.

# Chapter Eleven

The sunlight streamed through the dance studio's east window, making the hardwood floor gleam. Carrie stood in front of the mirror for her private lesson.

"Back straighter. Chin up," Kit said from her side, demonstrating the correct posture.

Her niece did exactly as Kit had said.

"Point your right toes more. That's good. Now take your bow." Kit had Carrie always bow at the end of the lesson.

Carrie whirled around, losing all the grace she fought to retain during her lesson, her expression lit. "How did I do? I think that was my best so far."

"You did great. You and I will have worked together almost four weeks. I promised your mom a demonstration at the end of a month, and I think you're going to dance beautifully for her."

"Yes." Carrie pumped her arm in the air. She blew Kit a kiss. "Gotta go. I'm going into town with Mom when she takes you to the dance academy." At the door her niece ran back, squeezed Kit in a tight hug, then darted out of the studio.

Lexie pranced into the room. She never came in when students were in here, but once they left, she always did.

"I still have a little time before I have to be at the dance academy. I want you to watch what I've been thinking about doing. I keep saying I can't do ballet steps. What if I can? Not performance level but maybe I can still execute a move well enough that someone could tell what it is."

Lexie cocked her head to the side as she listened to Kit.

"I'm going to try an attitude, then a pirouette. See if I can go from one move to another."

Kit faced the mirror to watch herself as she posed on her right leg, lifting her left, curved and at a ninety degree angle, then took two steps and went into a pirouette, twirling in a circle on the ball of her right foot with both arms curved above her head. Halfway around, she teetered and went down, her shoulder slamming into the hardwood.

She pounded her fist into the floor. Frustration flashed through her, hot and quick. She'd done those steps thousands of times. They had been second nature to her. Not anymore. Her mind wanted to do them. Her body didn't cooperate.

She hunched over, her forehead against the cool hardwood. She fought the overwhelming desire to bawl. She'd cried enough at what she'd lost. She had to stop giving in to tears. Now. Her palm banged against the floor again and again, pain shooting up her arm.

"Simple steps. Why can't I at least do those?"

A wet nose nudged her cheek. She turned her head and stared into Lexie's big brown eyes.

Her poodle whimpered.

"I'm all right, Lex. I had to try." She pushed herself to a sitting position and patted her lap.

Lexie hopped up and snuggled close to Kit.

"I'm going to try again and again until..." Until what? She gave up? She hurt herself? "Until I can at least go through the proper movements. Not perfectly. I don't have to be perfect anymore."

Lexie barked her agreement.

Later that day after dismissing her students, Kit slipped into Madame Zoe's class to wait for Anna, who would be instructed by both of them during the week. Kit sat, still not quite up to the energy level she wanted. She'd been teaching for over two weeks and thought by now she wouldn't be so tired on the days she taught Carrie, her friends and the students at the Summer Dance Academy, and then rehearsed with the teens for the Western shindig—now only nine days away. After all, as a dancer she'd been used to nonstop work. Often her life had revolved around it.

But exhaustion clung to her, and with a two-hour rehearsal ahead of her, she would have to dig deep to keep herself going.

"No. No, Anna." Madame Zoe's booming voice cut into Kit's thought. "You aren't concentrating on the steps enough. You're getting sloppy. The rest of you are dismissed."

The nine students filed out of the studio, a couple of them throwing Kit a relieved look as they passed her. Anna remained in the center of the room, her gaze briefly touching Kit's before returning to Madame Zoe.

"I know you're dancing in that little production for your church and rehearsing after you leave here. Perhaps doing that is taking your mind off what is important. We will be having a performance when the Summer Dance Academy is over, and when you're here I expect your concentration 100 percent or I'm going to have someone else dance the lead. Now, you're to do that series of steps until I'm satisfied you're giving me that 100 percent."

Anna dropped her head. "Yes, Madame Zoe."

After the tenth run-through, Anna faced Madame Zoe, tears shining in her eyes. "What am I doing wrong?"

"You tell me. That's part of being a dancer. You should know when you aren't performing to your peak potential. Again."

"But Kit is waiting—"

"That's what I mean," Madame Zoe said, her words spoken in quiet steel. "Your mind is on leaving, not dancing."

Kit glanced at the wall clock and realized Nate would be outside to pick up both of them. She rose. "Anna, don't worry. I'll be out in the hall when you're ready."

When Kit left, she heard Madame Zoe repeat the word she used to dread as a student—"Again." She trudged toward the main exit in front, remembering being there years ago, leaving class feeling a failure and not quite sure how to improve. Over the time since, she'd had teachers like Madame Zoe who drilled relentlessly and others who told her exactly what they expected and how to achieve it. She'd never been afraid of hard work, but after classes with instructors like Madame Zoe she'd often questioned why she wanted to be a ballerina.

She headed for Nate's truck parked in front. The smile that lit his whole face at the sight of her warmed her as she neared the vehicle. Howard's second truck was in the shop, so sometimes when Nate was through with work at the animal hospital early, he'd pick up Anna and her to take them to the ranch. While he helped Howard and a few other teens work on the barn, finishing up the transformation, she'd help the dancers rehearse the performance. Beth worked with the singers. She and her sister-in-law made a good team.

She opened the passenger door. "Anna has been delayed. Do you mind waiting?"

"Of course not. I remember waiting for you after some of your classes with Madame Zoe. Is it the same problem?"

"Yes, Anna isn't doing the steps the way Madame Zoe wants."

"And she isn't telling her why?"

"She hasn't changed over the years. I told Anna I would wait in the hallway."

Nate removed the keys from the ignition. "Then I'll keep you company."

But before he rounded the hood of the Silverado, Anna hurried out of the building. She got into the backseat while Kit slipped into the front one.

She glanced back at the teenage girl whose

blurry eyes and quivering bottom lip brought back memories of Kit's own trials. "I wish I could tell you it gets easier," Kit said gently. "It doesn't. Each instructor you have will demand something a little different from your last. In order to survive, you'll have to toughen yourself. They aren't criticizing you but your dancing. There's a difference."

"How? I *am* my dancing," Anna said in a thick voice as Nate climbed into the cab and started the engine.

"No, you're not. Dancing is important, but there's more to you than that." As Kit said those words, part of her was surprised because at Anna's age she hadn't thought that. Even six months ago she hadn't believed it. Her accident had forced her to look beyond her career to realize who she was without dancing. "It's okay to have other interests besides ballet."

"Did you?" Anna asked.

Nate slid a look toward Kit.

She shifted in her seat, rubbing her hands together. "No, and I'm regretting that now."

"Because of what happened?"

Anna's question made Kit even more uneasy. She knew some ballerinas who had boyfriends or husbands. Some that enjoyed hobbies in their downtime. Not her. "Yes. I had nothing to fill the hours of inactivity after my accident. Balance is important in a person's life, even a dancer's."

"I used to play the guitar, but lately I've stopped."

Kit peered over her shoulder at Anna. "Do you enjoy it?"

"Yes."

"You know we could use you to play something at the fund-raiser. Do you know any country-western songs?"

Anna's eyes brightened. "That's usually what I played. I haven't picked up my guitar in a year. Let me think about it."

"Sure."

Nate drove through the gates of the Soaring S Ranch and minutes later parked next to Kit's cabin. A few of the other performers were waiting on the porch. Anna hurried from the back.

As Kit placed her hand on the handle, Nate stopped her. "I got a call about our fund-raiser from the local television station. They wanted to do a spot about our Western shindig, especially after they heard you were involved. In fact, they want to interview you and film some of the rehearsal, then do a follow-up the night of the fund-raiser."

"When do they want to schedule the interview?" Kit managed to ask while the muscles in her stomach twisted and knotted.

"As soon as possible."

"How do they know about the shindig?"

"Pastor Johnson's neighbor is the evening news anchor."

"Do they know about my leg?"

"They didn't say anything about it."

Her fingers clutched the handle, her knuckles white. "How did they know about me?"

"When they asked about the shindig, I explained what we were doing. Your name came up in connection to the entertainment."

She stiffened. "Do they think I'll be dancing?"

He clasped her left hand. "I made it clear this was driven by the youth group. Their fundraiser for their mission trip. If you choose to meet with the reporter, it'll be your decision what you want to say. You've been fine when someone at church says something to you about your accident or your leg. Is this any different?"

It was one thing to talk about her prosthetic leg with people she knew, but totally different when strangers became involved. Her throat closed, she nodded, then shoved open the door and descended to the ground.

She heard Nate slam his door and then his footsteps behind her. When he caught up with her, she stopped and said to the group of six teens, "You all go inside and start warming up. I'll be there in a minute."

When the kids disappeared from view, she faced Nate. "We have a lot to do, especially if one of our rehearsals is going to be filmed for the evening news."

"It doesn't have to be. It's your call."

"But it would be great publicity for the fund-raiser."

"Yes," Nate admitted.

"Then I have no choice. I've gotten to know these teens and I want to help them help others. If we can raise more than needed for the Honduras trip, I've heard a few talk about some shorter trips, ones within Oklahoma. I like that. It makes me wish I had done some volunteering of my own at their age." She attempted to reassure Nate with a smile, but from his worried expression she didn't think it had worked. "I'll be fine. Now, I've got work to do. We'll be up at the barn later to block the dances on the stage."

He took her hands, holding them up between them as he edged closer. "Thank you. When I asked you last month about helping, I didn't think you would but I'm so glad you did. The group sees you working hard on this fund-raiser with what happened to you, and it spurs them to do as much as they can."

She squeezed his hand, then stepped back. "See you later."

As she entered her cabin, hearing the laughing and voices coming from the studio she created, she thought about what Nate had said about teens being inspired to work harder because of her. She was glad they were putting a lot into the fund-raiser, but she'd never thought of the loss of her leg as an inspiration to others.

Heading toward the back of the house, Kit felt overwhelmed with mixed feelings about her first media interview since the accident. She hadn't become a ballerina to be in the limelight. She'd loved using her body to tell a story, to provoke emotions in others, much like a writer used words.

*What's stopping me from doing that for myself?* That question stayed with her as she began class and ran through each of the routines, but no answer came.

"Nate, are you heading to the old barn?" Beth asked later that evening as she came out onto the porch of the main house.

"Yes, my truck is parked there. What do you need?"

"Carrie and Kit. Dinner is nearly ready. In fact, I hope you'll stay. I fixed enough to feed an army in case anyone was still up at the barn."

Howard shook his head. "Everyone has gone home. Steven left a few minutes ago. I saw his dad pick him up."

Beth frowned. "I'm assuming the man was driving at a safe speed."

"Yep, he even waved to Nate and me when he drove by."

Beth turned toward Nate. "So how are he and Steven getting along?"

"Better. They're talking. His dad still isn't happy that Steven quit football, but he isn't hounding him every day to reconsider."

"That's a step forward. Good for him. Forcing someone to do something is the quickest way to get them to hate whatever it is." Beth glanced between her husband and Nate. "What have you two been up to out here for the past half hour?"

"We've been discussing some publicity opportunities that have come our way, and giving my sister some space."

Beth's forehead crinkled. "Why does Kit need that? Everything looked fine when I left. Her dancers were going through the dance on stage."

"Until she got to the final performance. She isn't happy with how it appears on the stage. In her studio it was okay but apparently not now." Nate shrugged. "I thought it was great."

Howard laughed and clapped Nate on the

back. "She is a perfectionist when it comes to her dancing. She'll keep at it until it's where she wants it to be."

"And, Beth, you want me to go back there?"

She harrumphed. "Don't say a thing about what she's doing and you'll be fine. After all, my daughter hasn't run back to the house complaining."

"That's because Kit can do no wrong in Carrie's eyes. Plus she has the kid thing on her side. I don't." Nate started down the steps. "I'm going to need two helpings of your dessert for this."

"Sorry to disappoint you. I didn't make one this time."

He swiveled around and backpedaled. "What? No dessert? Surely I didn't hear right. You always have one."

"I'm going on a diet and that's one thing I'm cutting out, but you're still invited to dinner."

Nate chuckled and continued his mission to get Kit and Carrie for dinner. When he approached the barn, he slowed his pace and stopped at the entrance, peeking in to see what was happening before going inside.

While music from *Oklahoma* played, Kit was moving through the dance steps on the stage, half dancing as much as she could with her prosthetic leg. Carrie clapped over and over as Kit move through the piece. Red splotches tinted

Kit's cheeks, but she kept going. Then something happened. Her expression transformed from tension into contentment and a radiant glow shone through her eyes as though she'd become lost in the music playing and was back performing on the stage in New York. When she finished and came to a stop in the middle, she blinked, looked around and smiled.

Carrie ran to Kit and threw her arms around her. "You were great. I love watching you dance."

Kit blushed but squeezed her niece and kissed the top of her head. "You don't have to be great to dance and enjoy it. Lose yourself in the music and let your body go with the flow of it. What does it say to you? What emotions take over? Let them pour from you. You can't go wrong if you do. People will know it is coming from your heart."

Nate didn't want to eavesdrop anymore without Kit knowing he was there. He moved forward.

She glimpsed him and said, "Carrie, I suspect Nate has come to tell us dinner is ready. Why don't you go tell your mother I'm going to fix myself a sandwich then go to bed early."

"Okay, Aunt Kit, but she'll probably not be too happy."

"Tell her Nate is going to share a sandwich with me. That'll make your parents happy."

Carrie giggled and raced from the barn, giving Nate a grin as she went by.

"There goes my super fan." Kit made her way to her bag and removed a hand towel, then ran it over her face and neck. "You don't have to come to dinner at the cabin. I had to think fast, and that was the first thing I could think of that would get me off the hook."

Taking off his cowboy hat, he bowed, sweeping his arm across his body, then plopping his Stetson back on. "I'm glad I could accommodate you. Don't say I haven't helped you."

Gripping the hand railing, Kit descended the side stairs of the raised stage. "Never. You've helped me more than I had any right to ask."

"Why do you say that? We're friends, aren't we? Doesn't that give you the right to ask?"

"We both know we wouldn't have broken up years ago if I hadn't insisted. I'm the one who didn't have the time for a relationship."

He took her bag, then her hand, and started for the cabin. "Neither one of us was ready for that kind of commitment. You were right to end things between us. You don't have to fix me a sandwich. I can always throw something together at home."

"I know Beth. She asked you to eat with them.

I'm not depriving you of your food. That's the least I can do for using you as an excuse not to go to a family dinner. It's been a long day full of a lot of emotions I need to work my way through."

On her porch he turned to her, hooking her stray hair from her ponytail behind her ear. "Then that's my cue to leave you alone."

"No, please stay and keep me company at least through dinner. The one thing I've realized I need is someone to talk to about what's going on. In New York I cut myself off from my friends when I needed them the most. I don't want to make that mistake again."

"Okay, if you let me make the sandwich."

"You've twisted my arm, but fine. You can fix dinner." Kit opened the door. Right inside the entrance sat Lexie. Kit bent over and picked up her poodle, nestling her against her neck. "When I'm here, Lexie always has a way of making my problems go away for the time being. I've lived without an animal for a long time, but now I don't think I could anymore. You were so right about having a dog to help me."

"Chalk one up for my side." He drew a *1* in the air.

"While you're fixing sandwiches, I'm going to get more comfortable."

Before heading to the kitchen, Nate watched her cross to the hallway, dressed as she often was when taking classes, in a leotard and skirt, this one long. The foot of her prosthetic leg peeked out, clad in a ballet shoe matching her right one. Just standing before him, he couldn't tell anything was different until she walked. Her limp was more pronounced this evening.

Kit sat on her bed to remove her prosthetic leg, then went through an abbreviated care routine, which she would finish after Nate left. But for the time being, her left leg was sore, and she wanted to go without her prosthesis. She checked for any signs of irritation before cleaning the area and massaging the skin.

She could have waited until Nate left in an hour, but if a relationship was going to progress, he needed to see her without her prosthetic leg. She hadn't even shown her brother or Beth yet. For some reason, it seemed right to let Nate see first.

The realization she was falling in love with him again struck her like a bolt of lightning. For weeks she'd been telling herself he was only a friend, that their time had been when they were young and didn't know what a relationship really meant. Over the years she'd dated other dancers, and when those relationships hadn't worked out, she'd decided she wasn't supposed to fall in love and get married. But now Nate had her reconsidering. Yet was she really ready for a commitment when she still wasn't sure about her plans for the future?

After wiggling into a comfortable pair of knee-length shorts and a T-shirt, she snatched her crutch and stood at the side of the bed, steadying herself. Then she walked toward the open living area, her stomach solidifying. Her sweaty palms caused her crutch to almost slip from her support until she gripped it tighter.

The first thing she spied when entering from the hallway was the table set for two. Then she swung her attention toward the kitchen and caught Nate staring at her. Not in horror. Not in revulsion. His expression softened, his eyes gleaming.

His gaze stayed linked to hers as he crossed to her and cupped her face. "You're the most beautiful person I know—inside and out."

When he lowered his head and covered her mouth with his, it felt like what energy she had left drained from her, and she wrapped her right arm around him at the same time he wound his about her. His kiss possessed her, claiming her as his. Her crutch fell to the floor, and she depended on his support to stay upright.

In that moment she realized she wasn't just

falling in love with him—she'd already fallen. She loved him. When he leaned back to stare into her eyes, the words to tell him were on the tip of her tongue, but she swallowed them. She wasn't ready. It was still too new. She was still trying to figure her life out. She didn't want to hurt him again.

"What kind of sandwich did you make?" she finally asked when the intensity in his look was robbing her of rational thought.

"You're talking food after that kiss?"

"I burned a lot of calories today. First working with Carrie alone, then the dance academy and finally the rehearsal. I need nourishment." She prayed he couldn't see her newfound love in her face. Not yet. She pointed to her crutch. "Will you pick that up for me?"

He laughed. "I've got a better idea."

Suddenly he scooped her up into his arms and walked toward the table. A thrill shot through her at being carried in his embrace. Lexie yelped the whole way until Nate eased her into the chair kitty-corner from him. When he straightened, she missed his touch.

"Is Lexie going to chew my ankle or is she cheering us?" Nate took his seat.

"Cheering. She growls if she's upset or leery."

"Whew. That's good to know." Nate bowed his head and blessed the food, then dug into his roast beef sandwich. "Howard got a call from the reporter to set a date. She'd like to interview everyone and film the rehearsal as soon as possible. Would tomorrow at five be okay? The rest of us in the barn will be quiet while they're here. We want the piece shown as soon as possible, hopefully the Sunday evening news."

"I feel like I'm being steamrolled. We aren't completely ready, but the first dance is in good shape. We'll work on that one while they're here. I'm glad I told the kids it was a possibility." Kit took a bite of her food.

"How did they take it?"

"With excitement. On Tuesday and Thursdays I don't work as long with Madame Zoe, and Carrie and her friends' lesson with me will be through by three. When you leave, I'll give the cast a call to be here thirty minutes earlier than usual. That'll give us some extra time to prepare for the interview."

"Good. Beth will have her group here, too, although the interview will probably revolve around you."

"That's the part I don't like, but I guess I can use my situation to help with the publicity for the fund-raiser." Kit had come to that conclusion as she'd worked with some of the girls who didn't make the Summer Dance Academy. A few had been so discouraged but she was trying to show them there was more to life than ballet—and more to ballet than the Summer Dance Academy. Not making the cut, which had seemed so tragic to the girls at the time, had actually opened the door to having other experiences with their summer that they couldn't have managed if they'd attended the academy. She had to remember to see her own situation in the same light.

Nate frowned and lifted his glass to his lips to take a sip. "I don't want you to feel you have to put yourself on display."

"If I want to show these young people that tragedy doesn't mean the end of a dream I must be able to talk frankly about my experiences. I've found with Carrie and her friends that's the only way to make my point. Some of them were talking about not taking ballet anymore since they didn't get into Madame Zoe's academy. One of Carrie's girlfriends asked what's the point."

His expression evened out, and he relaxed in the chair. "How did you answer her?"

"We talked about interests and hobbies. We don't do them to become world famous or even to be on stage. We don't do them to make a lot of money. We do them because they bring us satisfaction and joy. Then I asked the girls why they took dance in the first place and if they enjoyed it while they did it. Each one said they loved it. They haven't said anything else about quitting since that first class. In fact, I'm having them do small parts in the performance, and they're excited about that."

Nate locked gazes with her. "You're a natural teacher. I saw that today while you were working with the kids on the stage."

"You think that's what I should do?" She'd considered it but wasn't sure.

"It's not what I think that matters."

She nibbled on her bottom lip, looking across the room at the wall where there was a photo of her performing in *Swan Lake*. "What if what I want is to dance? That's not going to happen."

"When I watched you earlier running through some steps, you were dancing. It won't be the same, but you can still do it."

"I know. I'm trying to give up the notion of performing in front of an audience. There is more to ballet than that. I've discovered—or rather rediscovered—that lately with the students I've been working with. And choreographing the performance for the fund-raiser has been challenging but fun. Both have given me something to do this summer. Otherwise, I would have gone crazy with boredom." Kit sipped her tea, part of her surprised by what she'd said. Until now she hadn't really stopped and thought about it. She did like to teach and choreograph—more than she had realized in New York. For the first time she glimpsed a future, not quite as she'd envisioned this time last year, but at least one involving ballet.

When Kit finished her dinner, Nate took the plates and glasses to the sink, then picked up her crutch and brought it to her at the table.

"I'd better leave. Tomorrow is going to be a long day. Just know I'll be there cheering you on during the interview." He glanced down at Lexie, now sitting in her lap. "Along with Lexie." He bent down and brushed his lips across Kit's. "I'll let myself out."

She watched him leave, stroking her dog, the action soothing. When she was alone, she held up Lexie. "I love him, but I also did when I was younger. I don't know what to do. Should I say something to him? Or should I keep quiet because it isn't fair to him to tell him, then leave like I did before? Lex, don't tell anyone, but I need to go back to New York. I left my life there unresolved."

Lexie snuggled against Kit's neck.

"Don't worry. I'll take you if I leave. I can't do it without you, girl."

## *Chapter Twelve*

A series of raps sounded at Kit's door the day of the Western Shindig the following week. She set her teacup on the counter and hurried to answer it. When she pulled it open, Beth rushed into the cabin, waving Cimarron City's newspaper.

"Your story is on the front page. You must have wowed the lady. First the television station and now the newspaper. When they get to the part about the fund-raiser, my name is mentioned." Beth grinned. "My fifteen minutes of fame."

"In my book you should get more. This fund-raiser is going to be a success tonight due to your hard work on the food and costumes."

"Oh, I almost forgot the other reason I came down here." Beth disappeared outside and when she came back in, she carried a bouquet of yellow roses. "I was tempted to peek at the card, but I didn't."

Kit knew who had sent her the yellow roses. Nate. He had done the same thing at her first professional performance and then her first one with the New York ballet company. That had been the only contact she'd had from him after they'd broken up. When Beth set them on the table, Kit plucked the card out of the greenery while her sister-in-law headed for the door.

"Where are you going?" Kit asked as she saw Nate's name sprawled across the white note.

"To get the other bouquet of flowers." She brought in an arrangement of deep red roses. "You're popular today."

"Nate sent the yellow ones. Who would send these?"

"I suggest you read this." Beth presented her with its card.

When Kit did, her hands shook as she stared at the name on it. Gordon Simms. The man who ran the New York ballet company. "My previous boss. How did he even know about tonight? Even if he somehow heard about the news story, flowers are something he'd send for a performance and no one knows I'm going to perform except you." Kit glanced at Beth. "You didn't tell anyone, did you?"

"No way. Maybe Madame Zoe said something to someone who told him. You've said the business is small and close-knit."

"I'll ask her when she comes tonight. We need to talk anyway. Lately I've put in my time at the Summer Dance Academy and left without saying much to her. With this performance tonight and the couple of extra classes I'm teaching, I haven't had a lot of time. I'm not sure how she feels about me teaching the girls who didn't get into her program. She may feel I'm infringing on her turf, but my methods are different from hers."

"And I appreciate it. Carrie gets so excited right before attending your class, and when she comes back, she's still excited and happy. That hasn't been that way for months with Madame Zoe."

Kit started to say she was only teaching the classes for a while longer, but another knock at the door cut her off before the first word was out. She peered at Beth. "Expecting anyone?"

Her sister-in-law shook her head, moving toward the entrance. "I'll get it. It might be Howard," she said as she opened the door, her eyes growing round. "Who are you?"

Kit covered the distance as quickly as she could. "This is Gordon Simms." She hugged him. "First these beautiful roses and now you. What are you doing here?"

Gordon, dressed in his usual attire of black pants and shirt, pulled back, clasping Kit's upper arms and assessing her. "You're looking great, and I'm here to see your production tonight and talk to you. Can't a person come to support a friend?"

"I know that look. There's more going on here."

Beth breezed by Kit, waving Gordon into the cabin. "I'm Kit's sister-in-law, Beth. Welcome to the Soaring S Ranch. I've got to go. So much to do. So little time."

"She's a whirlwind," Kit said with a laugh when Gordon was speechless as Beth scurried away.

He combed his fingers through his wild mass of white hair. "I want her energy." Scanning the living area, he moved farther into the room. "Cozy but not what I expected."

"What did you expect?"

"A Western theme. This is more eclectic than I thought."

"That's because it belonged to my grandparents, and they didn't care what kind of furniture they had. If they loved it, they added it to their home."

"Were they hippies in the sixties?"

The image of Granny and Papa as hippies

formed in her mind, and she burst out laughing. "The very opposite."

"You had very simple furniture in your apartment in New York. This is so..." He gestured in a flourish.

"Cluttered?"

"Right."

Kit crossed her arms over her chest. "Okay, cut the small talk. Why are you really here?"

Gordon's lips puckered together. "I came to see your production."

"And?"

"I wanted to wait until after the production to talk about this, but since you forced my hand, we'll talk now." Gordon strolled to the couch and sat, relaxing back.

Kit shook her head and took the chair across from him. "All right. You've piqued my interest." She narrowed her eyes on him. "But I think that was the object of the visit this morning."

He smiled. "You know me well, which is part of the reason I'm here to offer you a chance to choreograph a ballet for the company. There have been such rave reviews about the choreography in *Wonderland*..."

Kit tuned out the rest of his spiel. She couldn't get past his proposition.

"Kit, are you listening to anything I'm saying?"

He clapped his hands, and she totally focused

on him. "Sorry. Did I hear you correctly? You want me to choreograph a ballet for the company?"

"Yes, for the fall season. You're the one who wanted us to do a ballet about *Alice in Wonderland.* You came up with half the dances in that ballet. You're ready to do one by yourself. I'd like you to return to New York and help with others. Your creativity and knowledge of dance are what I've always admired about you."

"Not my dancing?"

"Don't get me wrong. You were a wonderful ballerina, or I would never have put you in a principal role."

*Were.* That word stood out, obliterating the rest of what he said. Again she was painfully reminded of the hard truth. It wasn't going to change. Tonight would be her goodbye dance. "Let me think about it. When are you leaving?"

"I'm staying through Monday because I promised Zoe I would be a guest teacher with a couple of her classes."

"I didn't know you and Zoe were good friends."

Shifting on the couch, Gordon lowered his look. "We started out in the same company and kept up with each other through the years long-distance. She's my date tonight to this Western Shindig."

Was something else going on? Why hadn't Madame Zoe said anything to her about knowing Gordon Simms so well? Had she been instrumental in Kit getting a job with the company in the first place? Doubts began to nibble at her composure. "Let me think about it. I'll tell you Monday after classes. It'll be fun to see you with the girls," she continued, shifting the topic so that Gordon couldn't press her for an answer. "Madame Zoe had hinted to the older girls that someone would visit soon, but she wouldn't tell them who. Or me."

"I asked her to keep it a surprise."

"Does she know you're asking me to choreograph for the company?"

"Yes. I didn't want to whisk her star teacher away without saying something to her."

Again doubts and something much more insidious began to attack her. Did Madame Zoe want her out of the way because she'd been working with Carrie and her friends as well as Anna?

Gordon rose and came to Kit. "I don't want to keep you from doing all the last-minute things I know need to be handled right before a performance. I'll see you tonight." He bent over and kissed her cheek. "I'll let myself out."

When the door clicked shut, the silence she'd craved when she first got here taunted her. She stared at the photograph hanging on the wall of her at another time in her life. *Father, I don't know what to do. Please help me.*

Would He answer this plea? He'd been so quiet while she'd been in New York in her apartment, wrestling with all she was going through.

During the intermission, Nate stood at the back double doors into the barn watching the sun starting to set. Streaks of rose, orange and purple layered the horizon and branched outward into the darkening blue. A light breeze cooled the air.

Howard came up to Nate, pushing his cowboy hat up on his forehead. "Don't tell my wife this or she'll think I'm a sentimental guy, but I often come here at the end of the day to watch the sun go down. This is one of the best places to see it at the ranch. We do have beauties here in Oklahoma."

"Your secret is safe with me. And I agree with you. While working here in the evenings, I've paused to come out here and take a moment to appreciate God's wonders."

"I can't believe how many people showed up for this fund-raiser. Many aren't even family or relatives of our kids, but then we had some great publicity. You and the youth group will be able to do a couple of mission trips."

"The publicity started with the television interview Kit had and got better and better. Look at the film crew. Kit's interview went so well that they came back here for the follow-up."

Howard looked toward the stage. "I see Beth signaling me. Intermission is over."

Nate decided to stay in the back to watch the scenes from *Oklahoma* being performed. He knew how much this meant to Kit, and he prayed everything went smoothly. She'd put her heart into this production.

The first group of teens came out onto the stage with the backdrop of the Oklahoma prairie and cattle grazing in the tall grass. Nate's heartbeat raced with anticipation and trepidation. What if… He shook the doubts away.

After each dance and song, the audience cheered and applauded. Nate joined in, putting two fingers in his mouth and blowing a loud whistle. The final performance with each group participating in the song "Oklahoma" brought the people to their feet. The teens took a bow, and then Anna, the lead dancer, moved forward. The crowd slowly quieted and sat again at their round tables.

"I am honored to introduce the last performance of the night. It's not in your program so it could be a wonderful surprise. Kathleen Somers will dance in her final ballet of her career. Dance can be enjoyed by all, as you will see." Anna swept her arm toward the side of the stage.

Kit came out in a long flowing white skirt that hit her at midcalf. He sucked in a deep breath. With her chin lifted, she positioned herself in the center of the stage, the elegance of her long arms and graceful hands pulling his attention away from her legs. Until she moved. As she flowed across the floor, he slowly released the trapped air in his lungs, marveling at the beauty of her steps. He found himself enthralled by the poetry of her dance to *Madame Butterfly*'s "Un Bel Di Vedremo," her heart in each movement, the thrill and joy on her face as the piece came to an end.

His throat swelled. Through a shimmering blur, he watched her take her bow to a stunned audience. One second. Two. Then the clapping began and a thunderous standing ovation erupted.

Transfixed, Nate sniffed and added his applause. Every time he saw her perform he was in awe of her ability. He understood now what she had gone through after the accident. Ballet was part of her. How do you give that up?

As she accepted a bouquet of flowers from the teens, he closed his eyes, holding the sorrow and joy inside. For the first time he questioned God and why He allowed the ability to perform professionally to be taken away from Kit. He turned away from the stage and stared at the darkness beyond the back doors.

Surrounded by the teens, Kit finally started backstage to make way for the square dancing to begin. But not before she'd seen Nate turn away. Had her performance upset him? Disgusted him? She'd had to modify the steps and rely more on her arms than the choreography usually called for, but she wanted to convey the emotions of love and sadness the song from *Madame Butterfly* evoked.

"Thank you all for doing such a great job tonight. I suggest you all change and go out and enjoy square dancing. It's fun." Kit swept her gaze around the group.

"How about you?" Anna asked as the kids dispersed.

"I've danced enough today. I'm going to enjoy watching you all." *Where is Nate?*

Anna turned to leave, stopped and swung back around. She gave Kit a hug. "You did great."

*I'm not going to cry. I've done enough of that to last two lifetimes.*

Kit gulped. Quickly she headed for her makeshift dressing room, a stall, to change. She'd needed to prove to herself she could do one last dance on her terms. She had. But why had Nate looked away?

She dressed in her jeans and a Western shirt with fringe, checked herself in the mirror, then parted the curtains to leave.

Nate stood outside, his shoulder cushioned against the wall. His eyes skimmed over her, and he gave a wolf whistle. He came to her.

She started to step away, still remembering his back to her as she skimmed the audience at the end. But she allowed him to grasp her hands and hold them up between them as he moved even closer. "What did you think?" Her lungs seized her next breath.

"Granted I'm not a ballet expert, but that was the most beautiful dance I've ever seen. Watching the emotions behind your moves was stunning." His voice heavy and thick, he swallowed hard.

"So I didn't make people uncomfortable?" *I didn't make* you *uncomfortable?*

"Were you in the same place I was? Did you hear the applause at the end?"

His slow smile that reached deep into his eyes cloaked her in a sense of finality—ending one chapter in her life and beginning a new one. "Yes, but I wondered if they were just being kind."

"Not from what I saw on their faces and their enthusiastic response to your performance. They, like myself, knew they were viewing something extraordinary. It brought tears to my eyes. Good tears." He inched even closer until nothing separated them. "That couldn't have been easy for you."

"One of the hardest things I've ever done, but if I can't perform, I can at least help others not give up on something they love because of a setback. These past weeks I've realized I can dance, even if I can't perform. I don't have to give up what I love totally. I'll enjoy it differently."

Right before his mouth settled on hers, she glimpsed a look on his face that stole her breath. Their lips touching sent a wave of goose bumps down her length. She lost herself in his kiss, savoring his embrace, his scent, his taste.

Someone coughed, the sound penetrating the haze of sensations engulfing Kit. She pulled back and looked around Nate to spy Madame Zoe. Heat seared Kit's face.

Nate turned, glanced from Madame Zoe to Kit. "I'll leave you two. I promised Beth I would dance once with her for making her special brownies."

When he left, Madame Zoe closed the space between herself and Kit. "Gordon told me what he offered you this morning. Are you going to go back to New York?"

Debra and Steven came around the corner, both grinning at Kit. She nodded toward them, then parted the curtain into the makeshift dressing room. "Let's talk in here where we won't be interrupted."

Madame Zoe swept into the converted stall as though she was entering a dressing room at the Metropolitan Opera. Kit entered behind her.

"I haven't decided what I'm going to do for sure. He only asked this morning."

Her mentor swung around, her head held high. "How can you pass up an opportunity like that? When he mentioned it to me, I thought it would be perfect for you, especially given what you did with this little fund-raiser and raw talent."

"Anna isn't a newbie."

"She still has a lot to learn, as you did at her age."

"Have you ever told her what she's doing right?" Remembering her own years with Madame Zoe, Kit doubted it, but she had always kept at it even without praise or encouragement. She had wanted to learn so badly, and Madame Zoe was the best available in the area.

"If I don't say something is wrong, then it's

right. If she doesn't have to redo it, then it's an acceptable step. That's a given."

"But it's nice to hear the words every once and a while."

"I'm not here to pamper kids. I'm here to teach them the *correct* way to dance." Her mentor's mouth slashed into a frown. "You never complained about my methods before."

"Because I didn't know anything different. But since I left Cimarron City, I've had various teachers, some like you and some who tell a dancer both the good and bad. When I think back on all my experiences, I flourished under the ones who told me what I did right and what I needed to work on. Each has value in teaching a person."

One of Madame Zoe's thin eyebrows arched. "And you know this after teaching for a month?"

"You called Gordon about what was happening here. Are you upset because I'm working with some students on the side here at the ranch? These past several weeks you and I don't talk like we used to. I didn't offer to work with the kids to offend you. They wanted to continue their dancing during the summer, and there wasn't a place for them in the dance academy."

She moved a couple of feet toward Kit. "I called Gordon because I think you should be in New York. You can become a top choreographer. I taught you all you need to know, and if you don't take his offer, you'll be blowing a great opportunity to keep yourself immersed in the ballet community. Isn't that what you want and love? You can't get that in Cimarron City."

A suspicion nibbled at her thought. "Why is it so important to you what I choose?"

Thunder descended over Madame Zoe's features. "Because *I* spent years honing your skills. You wouldn't be who you are if it wasn't for me."

Kit straightened, her shoulders back. "I beg your pardon. I did the work. Hours and hours every day for years. Yes, I learned from you but also from others. What really happened to your own career?" She bit the inside of her mouth to keep any other words inside, but her own anger festered in the pit of her stomach.

"I reached the soloist level and knew I wouldn't go any further. I was thirty-six and younger girls than me were becoming principals in the company. My window of opportunity to excel had closed."

"I never thought of you as giving up" came out of Kit's mouth before she could censure herself.

Madame Zoe blinked several times. "I'm a realist."

"There's nothing wrong with that. I'm a realist, too, so what I decide for myself will be what I think I should do realistically."

"All I ask is that you not be afraid to try something. If it doesn't work out, then fine. No regrets."

"Regrets? You sound like you're coming from experience. What kind have you had?"

Madame Zoe's expression softened into sadness. "There was a time I could have been a principal of a small relatively unknown ballet company, but I decided I wanted to stay in the bigger, more established one and try harder to become a principal dancer. Gordon urged me to take the role with the smaller company. I should have listened to him. You should listen to him now."

In that moment Kit realized Madame Zoe had dealt with her own heartache. Her anger dissolved. She didn't see her mentor through rose-colored glasses now, but she acknowledged that her teacher had contributed to her success and wanted what was best for Kit.

She stepped forward and wrapped her arms around Madame Zoe. "Thank you for recognizing raw talent all those years ago and working with me. You and I might not agree on everything, but I do know I'm in your debt. I'll let you know what my decision is when I make it."

Kit left the dressing room with Madame Zoe. They parted ways when they entered the main part of the barn. Kit noticed Nate still in the middle of a square dance with Beth. Then she saw Steven at the back of the stage with his dad. With the last day's hectic schedule, she hadn't had a chance to compliment Steven on how well everything with the scenery had turned out.

She mounted the stairs to the raised platform and skirted Bud at the front making the square dancing calls. All the dinner tables had been moved to the side so there was room in the middle of the barn for the people who wanted to participate in the dances.

"Hello, Steven, Mr. Case."

The older man smiled over his shoulder as she approached. "Daniel, please."

"I came over to tell you, Steven, what a talent you have for painting." Her arms rigid at her sides, Kit prepared herself for Daniel's disapproval. "I felt like we stepped back in time to when Oklahoma was becoming a state. You captured the prairie and farm perfectly. You've made a good choice taking art classes next year."

"Dad just said the same thing."

Kit swung her attention to Steven's father.

"You see why we were so happy he volunteered to do the scenery."

"Yes. I'm proud of what he did here. I still hope Steven will play some kind of team sport, though."

"Dad and I are talking about being in a father-son softball league next summer."

Daniel clasped his son around the shoulders. "It's for fun, but it will be nice to do it together."

Steven beamed, especially when a woman joined them, studying the backdrop.

"Who painted this?"

"I did, Mrs. Adams."

"Have you taken any art classes?"

Steven shook his head.

"You have a lot of potential. I hope to see you in one of my classes in the fall."

"You will—I signed up for one."

The woman's face brightened. "I'm glad. The students I think have potential I push to do even better. I hope you're ready for that."

"Yes, ma'am."

Kit left the three talking on stage and scanned the area around her. She needed to sit. All of a sudden, what adrenaline had gotten her through her solo had evaporated, leaving behind exhaustion. She made her way through the crowd watching the dancers in the center, and escaped outside. The cool breeze caressed her skin but didn't revive her. She started for her cabin.

"Kit, wait up," Nate shouted behind her.

Rotating toward him, she watched him through half-lowered eyelids, her limbs feeling as if they weighed twice their weight. "Only if you promise to see me home and then leave. I need to crash. I think the last few weeks are catching up with me, all in the last five minutes."

Nate looped his arm around her waist and pressed her against him, then strolled toward the cabin. As they walked, he commented on the cars parked in every place possible. "We had to have at least three hundred people here, especially earlier with the light supper and production."

"I'm glad." The reply barely formed on her tongue. Kit rested her head against him, feeling as though she were sleepwalking. She heard Nate talking about the night but the meaning of the words barely registered.

Nate held Kit upright, bearing most of her weight as he neared her house. She'd been pushing herself for the past week, sleeping little and doing more physical work than usual. She had to be worn out. On the porch, he started to open her door but decided to sit with her on the porch swing. Usually Kit could rest, then pick up where she left off.

He cuddled her against him. "Relax. You've been doing a lot. Rest for a little bit. Then I'll make sure you get inside."

She went slack next to him. The light from her living room cast a soft glow that illuminated her face. Her eyes closed, she appeared to be asleep. He could sit here and let her sleep for a while, but she'd be more comfortable sleeping in bed. Besides, he needed to get back to the barn. He was on the cleanup crew.

He cradled her across him and surged to his feet. When he walked to the front door with her in his arms, he fumbled for the handle and pushed into the cabin. Lexie greeted them with her happy bark. He looked at the couch and decided to take her to her bedroom.

In it, he gently placed her on the bed, then pulled a folded blanket off a chair and spread it over her. He stared at her for a long moment, her beautiful features arranged in a serene expression. Leaning over her, he kissed her cheek, then left the cabin.

Out on the porch, as car after car streamed away from the barn, a troubled thought kept pecking at his composure. From Beth he knew Kit's old boss had come all the way from New York to see her today and was at the production tonight. Why? Why didn't she say anything to him? Was her old boss asking her to return to New York? And now that the fund-raiser was over...would she go?

# *Chapter Thirteen*

Kit paced her dance studio, restlessness driving her from one end to the other. She'd told Gordon she would give him her answer by tomorrow. At church this morning, she'd finally asked God to help her. She still didn't know what to do. Always before, she'd been certain in her decisions, even when she decided to break up with Nate years ago. Her life had revolved around her ballet and she'd made whatever choice would help her in her career. Now that that wasn't a factor, it wasn't as clear how she should decide.

Chewing on her thumbnail, she came to a stop in front of the mirrored wall. Was she ready physically to dive back into a full-time job choreographing for her old ballet company? Could she be satisfied watching others take her creations and dance them? Instantly she recalled the moment last night when she observed Anna performing her solo. The sense of satisfaction of a job well done had blanketed Kit then, giving her the courage to go through with her final performance at the end.

Lowering her hand to her side, she stared at herself in the mirror. She felt so much stronger than she had been when she'd arrived seven weeks before. She knew what she needed to do.

Quickly she changed into her riding clothes and headed for the barn. Bud went out into the paddock and brought Cinnamon to her. After saddling and mounting her mare, she rode toward the ridge. She hadn't made it to the top by herself yet, but the last time she'd been with Nate they had gone most of the way. It was time to see if she could make it. It had become a personal test to show if she was ready to move on and start a new life.

At the bottom of the hill, she tipped her head back and peered up at the top. *I can do this by myself.* Before she was injured, she'd been able to scale the rise because she had been in top physical shape. She wasn't in the same condition now, but she was still strong and active. There were amputees who climbed mountains. They hadn't let their loss stop them from doing what they enjoyed.

She inhaled a composing breath and started. *I can do this with Your help, Lord. Anything is possible through You.* She kept repeating that as she ascended the mount.

Half an hour later, with only one slip, she reached the top, dragging herself over the ledge to stand on the ridge and stare down at the ranch.

"I made it," she shouted to the world, realizing as she scrambled up the hill that she had focused on the Lord, imagining Him with her each step. She hadn't been alone, but she had made it by herself.

She sank to the ground, drawing deep inhalations to fill her lungs. Swiping her hand across her sweat-coated forehead, she smiled as if she'd scaled Mount Everest. She'd challenged herself and won. She knew what she needed to do.

Nate parked near Kit's cabin and rapped on the door. No answer. Maybe she was up at the main house. He headed that way but decided to stop and see if she went riding. The day was perfect for it with a mild temperature and a light breeze. For Oklahoma June had been surprisingly pleasant. He wouldn't mind riding himself.

Nate saw Bud in the tack room and asked, "Have you seen Kit?"

"Yep, about half an hour ago."

"Which way did she go?"

"Toward the ridge."

Suddenly he knew what Kit was doing. He shouldn't be surprised because she always worked hard to accomplish what she had set out to do and climbing the ridge had become a challenge to her. But she'd agreed she shouldn't go to the top alone. What if she was at the bottom trying to decide what to do?

"Bud, can I saddle up Dynamite and take him to meet Kit?"

"Sure. I'm glad you're checking on her, but I knew it was useless to say anything to her. Strong-minded is a good description of Kit."

"As I well know."

Within ten minutes Nate rode toward the ridge, and when he arrived, he looked up to see Kit waving down at him from the top. Relief cooled some of his anger that she'd gone up by herself and hadn't called him to join her for the climb.

He started up the rocky incline. When he reached the top and hoisted himself over the ledge, he glared at Kit who sat on a stone smugly waiting for him. "What happened to the promise you made me? You said you wouldn't come up here alone." Nate hovered over her.

She craned her neck and regarded him with

an expression of satisfaction. "I wasn't alone. God was with me the whole way, and I made it. I slipped once but didn't go down. I caught myself."

"What if you hadn't?" he asked, his irritation slowly defusing. How could he be mad or argue with her when she pointed out the Lord was beside her?

"That's not important because it didn't happen."

Then Nate realized why he was upset with her even though she was safe. *He'd* wanted to be the one with her as she climbed the ridge. She had almost made it the last time she'd tried. He'd wanted to see the triumph on her face when she finally reached the top. Any hint of anger left drained completely from him, and he settled in next to her.

"I hate your logic," he grumbled.

She shrugged. "You were busy. I didn't want to wait. But I'm okay. Actually more than okay. I've come to a decision about my future. At least my immediate future."

The way she said it, he was sure that he wasn't going to like what she had decided. It probably had to do with Gordon Simms's visit. Dread solidified his gut. He placed his palms on the ground behind him and leaned back. "What are your plans?"

"Gordon Simms, who is the head of the New York ballet company I danced with, came to visit me yesterday morning. He had a proposition for me."

She paused as though to gather her thoughts on what to tell him. Nate's lungs burned, and he realized he'd been holding his breath waiting for her to break the news.

She twisted to look at him. "He wants me to help with the ballet company and choreograph a dance for him for the fall. I've been thinking how much I'd love to do one that interested both adults and children like the *Nutcracker* does at Christmas. That's what I loved about *Wonderland.* I've been thinking of coming up with one based on Mother Goose's nursery rhymes or the Grimm brothers' fairy tales. Create a world from various ones and tell a fun story that all people can relate to."

Excitement flushed her cheeks a rosy shade. As she talked about what she would do, he felt her slipping away from him again. "So what are you going to do?"

"I need to go back to New York. I have unfinished business there and want to see it through to the end." She gave him a grateful smile. "When I came to the ranch, I really had nowhere else to go to heal. It wasn't happening in

New York. But now I feel so much more hopeful for the future, thanks to you and my family."

Nate was whisked back eight years ago when she had broken up with him and told him she wanted him to find someone who would make him happy. He hadn't been able to bring himself to say that *she* was the one who made him happy, not when he knew she'd pick her ballet dreams over him. He had let Kit go without a fight. And he needed to do that again. She'd never belonged to him or his world. Finally he realized that.

She searched his expression, reaching out and touching his face, but he flinched and pulled back even further. "I've let you down again. I didn't mean to, but if I don't do this, I'll always wonder what I was capable of doing. These past weeks here I've loved working with the students and making up dances for them."

"Then stay and do that," he said and wanted to snatch those words back. He would not beg her to remain. It wouldn't work if he did. Why had he fallen for her all over again? He should have known this was how things would end.

"And do what? Teach a couple of classes a week? I need more. I've worked for years, long hours. I can't just stop all of a sudden and be content."

"I never said not to work, but to do it here.

Work with Madame Zoe or by yourself. You can still be part of the dance world. When you first came here, I was one of the people who tried to convince you that you could be involved with ballet."

"I know, but I feel like I was a quitter. I was so busy feeling sorry for myself I didn't look at the options I might have in New York. And, anyway, I have to go back in July because of my apartment. The person subletting is leaving. I'll have to make a decision then. I'm going to tell Gordon what I plan and leave not long after the Fourth of July. I'm choreographing a few dances for the performance at the end of the Summer Dance Academy. I should have them complete by then for Madame Zoe."

"What about Lexie?"

"I'm taking her with me. My neighbors have a dog, so I know my apartment building allows them. She's been there for me when I'm down and sad. I couldn't leave her behind."

*And yet you can me.* Nate rose. "Are you ready to go back?"

"No, I'm going to stay for a while."

"Then I'll stay, too."

She slanted a look at him. "Go back. I'm fine. You don't have to protect me."

He ground his teeth together.

"Please."

"Fine. I'll leave you alone."

Nate began his descent, having no intention of riding back to the barn. He would wait below until she came down. He would never be able to forgive himself if he left, and she hurt herself descending, which was more difficult than going up to the top.

Although Kit wasn't positive what she would do in the long run, taking Lexie with her told him her answer. New York was her home. She wouldn't be returning again. He should have known better than to trust her with his heart. Ballet would always come first in Kit's life, and he wasn't going to fight that fact anymore.

Carrie plopped down on Kit's couch and crossed her arms, a pout on her face. "You can't leave. I want you to keep teaching me. So do the other girls." She scooped up Lexie and began to stroke her over and over. "If you go, that means I'll have to go back to Madame Zoe's."

Beth came into the living room from the back of the cabin, pulling two of Kit's big suitcases. "No, you don't. I'll find another teacher who teaches like your aunt does."

Carrie glared narrow-eyed at Kit as she made her way to Lexie with the dog carrier. "I want her to stay here. I don't want to lose Lexie, too."

Beth snorted. "Quit being dramatic."

"Sorry, Carrie. Lexie is coming with me. Your mom said something about getting you a dog from Nate. They have strays dropped at the animal hospital from time to time."

"Is Nate driving you to the airport?" the girl asked, kissing Lexie goodbye.

"No, your dad is." Except across the church, she hadn't seen Nate since the day she told him about returning to New York. "Do you want to come, too?"

Carrie lifted her chin and looked away. "No. I don't want to say goodbye."

"Carrie, that's enough. Your aunt has to do what's best for her."

"Why? She comes here and shows me how much fun dance can be and then leaves."

"I thought you loved ballet." Kit zipped up the dog carrier.

"I wanted to be like you but..." Carrie flounced to her feet and stomped toward the door. "It doesn't make any difference what I like or think."

When the child left, Kit started to go after her.

"Leave her be. She'll get over her anger. Just give her time."

Kit rotated toward Beth. "I hear disappointment in your voice. With me or Carrie?"

"Both." Beth went back to the bedroom and brought the third piece of luggage out.

"Don't make me feel any worse than I do."

"Then don't go. It must mean something if you feel bad about leaving."

"I have to do this."

"Why?" Beth folded her arms over her chest, much like her daughter had earlier.

"If I don't, I'll always wonder if I could have made it if I'd been willing to try. I can't move on without knowing that answer." Needing to leave and not wanting to have this conversation with Beth, Kit moved toward the door.

"Do you love Nate?"

Beth's question halted Kit's progress. All night that was all she thought about. Yes, she loved him, had never really stopped loving him. But was it enough? She was scared. Dance was all she'd known for so long—she knew what was expected of her in ballet. If she stayed, she didn't know what to expect. She didn't like change and the chance to work with the ballet company and choreograph would be the closest work she could have to her former life.

"Sometimes a person has to consider more than love," she finally answered her sister-in-law.

"God gave us the ability to love because it's so important to have. It's what makes life worth living. I know you loved what you were doing, but there's more to life than work. Don't lose yourself in it and forget what's really important. We're here for you if you need us."

Tears obscured her view as Kit continued her trek outside where Howard should be waiting for her. But instead Nate had parked his truck at the end of the sidewalk.

He lounged against the side, but when he spotted her, he pushed away from the Silverado and strode toward her. "Howard had something come up and asked me to take you to the airport." He took two suitcases from Beth, who hugged Kit then scurried toward the main house. He set them in the back of his pickup, then returned to the porch for the last piece of luggage.

If she had the time and wouldn't be late for her plane, she'd find her brother and have a few choice words with him. He wouldn't give up his silly matchmaking plans. He thought he knew what she needed. Irritated, she hoisted her dog carrier onto the seat and then hauled herself up next to Lexie.

When Nate sat behind the steering wheel and started the engine, his hard expression emphasized the angular planes of his face. He pulled away from the cabin.

"You could have refused my brother." She

didn't want to leave with such anger between her and Nate.

"I know exactly what Howard is up to, but maybe he's right. Maybe we do need this time to finally say what needs to be said." He stopped at the gate and shifted toward her. "I love you. Does that mean anything to you?"

"Yes. I love you, but I need to do this."

"Because your career is the most important thing to you?"

"Because it has been who I am for most of my life ever since I was five and took my first ballet lesson. I have to see this through."

"I never asked you to give up dance. I'm willing to compromise."

"Would you be happy in New York? You love what you're doing and where you are."

"Yeah, and until you showed up, I was perfectly content with my life." He put the truck into Drive. "You're right. New York isn't for me. But mostly our relationship wouldn't work because I need to feel more than second place in your life. I've finally realized that my love doesn't mean the same as yours."

The rest of the trip to the airport passed in silence. A silence that made it difficult for Kit to pull her thoughts together. Was she making a mistake?

Nate parked and helped her bring her suitcases to the airline counter. After she checked in, she turned to find him gone. A sharp pain sliced through her heart as though she were leaving part of it in Oklahoma.

As Kit approached the intersection where she had her accident nearly nine months ago, she slowed her gait, clutching the strap of her purse. Sweat popped out on her forehead and drenched her palms. For three months since she'd returned to New York, she'd avoided this area. But she wouldn't hide from it today. This was one last hurdle she needed to overcome—the last remnant of her fear. She'd faced the fear of being part of the ballet company in a different role. It had proven to be fulfilling, but even after three months she knew that something was missing in her life. At first, she kept thinking it was the regret she couldn't perform and dance anymore, but over time she began to doubt that was the problem. Maybe this was it.

She stopped at the curb, a trembling in her hands spreading through her body. When the light indicated she could cross the street, she stood frozen while people flowed around her and into the intersection. Someone bumped her arm, and she nearly fell forward. She caught herself, sucking in gulps of air to quiet her thundering heartbeat.

She moved out of the stream of people and waited through the light changes. She wished Nate were here with her, holding her hand, giving her his support.

*Lord, I need to do this. Please.*

Two women nearby looked at her, and Kit wondered if she had said that prayer out loud. She didn't care. She wasn't going to do this without some help and Nate wasn't here.

As the walk sign flashed, a cloak of peace fell over her shoulder and cocooned around her. She stepped off the curb and fell into step with the crowd around her. When she made it to the other side, only a block away from where the performance of her first solo choreographed ballet would be tonight, she didn't know how she did it. She nearly collapsed to the sidewalk but grasped a pole close by and waited until she knew she could walk the length of the street to the theater to meet with Beth and Carrie. Her sister-in-law had brought her niece for the opening performance.

Carrie saw Kit and ran through the throng to hug her. "I wish you could have gone sightseeing with us today."

"I will tomorrow. There were last-minute things that needed to be done." Interestingly she'd never thought of asking Beth and Carrie to come with her when she crossed the street, even though she knew she'd have asked Nate if he were there. "You two will have my undivided attention then."

Beth finally caught up with her daughter. "If it were humanly possible, Carrie would have climbed that building over there. She has been so excited she can barely contain herself."

"We're going to go in through the stage door. This way." Kit gestured toward the alleyway between two buildings.

Carrie skipped ahead of them.

Beth chuckled. "She'd on cloud nineteen."

"How are the dance lessons with Madame Zoe?"

"Fine. About her ” Beth glanced away then back at Kit " she came on the same flight we did. Gordon Simms invited her to this opening."

"He did? He didn't say anything to me."

"I think he's been talking to her a lot since he came for the Western Shindig."

"You know this is beginning to make sense to me. I wondered why he didn't just call me about the job opportunity. Why come all the way to Cimarron City?" Continuing toward the backstage door, Kit lowered her voice because Carrie waited for them before going inside. "I thought maybe Madame Zoe had told Gordon about the production to get me out of town. That wasn't it. She wanted him to come see me, and see her, as well. Ah, she is crafty."

"Maybe she's tired of being alone. A career won't keep you warm at night."

Beth's words kept repeating themselves through the ballet performance and even the party afterward. Kit couldn't rid her mind of the fact she wasn't content even in the midst of the critical acclaim for her new ballet and the thundering applause from the audience. Taking her bow on stage as the choreographer had been a thrill, but the moment she left, that feeling fled to be replaced with emptiness. Several of her friends had gotten her flowers to congratulate her, but all she wanted was the bouquet of yellow roses from Nate that wasn't there.

Kit hugged first Carrie then Beth as the cabdriver finished putting their luggage in the trunk. "I had so much fun seeing New York through you-all's eyes yesterday."

As Carrie climbed into the backseat, Beth said, "I hope you'll be coming home for Christmas as usual, but you know the cabin is always there for you and you have a home on the ranch." She grinned. "After all, you are a part owner in it."

"I'll keep that in mind."

Kit waved to both of them as the cab drove

away. When it disappeared around the corner, tears coursed down her cheeks. They were gone one minute, and she already missed them. She'd missed them in the past when she'd left to return to New York, but not like this. She rubbed a fist into her chest where her heart ached.

By the time she reached her apartment, the wet streaks running down her face had increased. She scooped up Lexie, sank onto the couch and held her pet against her. "Lex, what am I going to do? I can't ignore it any longer. My life isn't the same as it was before. I'm different. I can't define myself as a ballet dancer any longer. I don't even want to anymore. What am I?"

She'd made a big mistake by walking away from Nate a second time. He forgave her the first time. How could she expect him to again? While in Oklahoma, she hadn't seen he was the best thing for her. She'd been too focused on her problem, and she'd hurt him.

Kit held her poodle up in front of her face. "Lexie, what should I do? Stay here?" She paused a few seconds. "Or go home?"

Lexie barked.

Nate sat at his desk in his office at Harris Animal Hospital, staring out the window. Colorful leaves swirled through the air, the wind whisking them down the street. The grayness of dusk settled over the landscape. What was Kit doing right now? A question he asked himself every day—even though he tried not to, because Kit would invade his thoughts. He remembered her last dance. The emotions she'd summoned that night could still rise into his throat.

A rap on his door frame followed by Emma poking her head into the room snagged his attention. He sent Emma a smile, appreciating the interruption. Thinking about Kit wasn't helping him move on.

Emma planted herself in front of his desk, one balled hand on her waist. "I thought you were having dinner at the Soaring S Ranch. If you don't get a move on it, you'll be late."

"It seems like when you're working, your personal mission is to make sure I leave at a decent hour." Nate pushed to his feet, wishing he hadn't agreed to dinner with Howard after putting in a twelve-hour day.

"That's because you're spending way too much time here. You're putting everyone else to shame for going home at a normal time. I heard Dr. Harris grumbling about that the other day."

"He did?"

"He said something about taking in a third partner. You're out there generating so much work for you two. The ranches in the next county are clamoring for your services."

"That's because the vet over there doesn't specialize in big animals like I do."

"And you're much better than he is, especially personality wise. Even animals respond to your kindness over his grumpiness. Speaking of going to the Somerses, have you heard how Lexie is doing with Kit?"

Where did that question come from? Nate shook his head and snatched up his keys on the desktop. "What does the vet in the other county have to do with the Somerses?"

"We were speaking of your dinner date and it made me think of Kit."

"All I've heard is what Beth told me last month when she returned from New York. Lexie has settled in well with Kit in her apartment. Carrie got a kick out of taking Lexie to the dog park nearby. She didn't realize they existed in big cities."

"What did Beth and Carrie say about the *Grimms' Tales?*"

"Since when have you been interested in ballet?"

"Since I met Kit. Besides, Madi talks about her all the time."

If he didn't leave soon, he would be late for dinner and he knew Emma wouldn't let him depart without an answer. She was like a bulldog. She wouldn't let go until she got what she wanted. "They raved about it. Apparently it's a huge success." He wouldn't add that he'd been following the stories about the ballet Kit had choreographed on the internet. If he was fool enough to mention that, then he'd be here until midnight with Emma bombarding him with one question after another. "Now, as you pointed out, I'm going to be late if I don't get a move on it."

When he walked outside, a cold wind from the north blasted him. Summer was definitely gone in Oklahoma. He shrugged into a jacket he'd left in the truck, then headed toward the ranch to his once-a-week dinner ritual with the Somers family. Although he enjoyed cooking, they had decided to take him under their wings and feed him. This needed to be the last time. How was he going to get Kit totally out of his mind if he kept going back to the ranch and seeing the cabin?

Darkness covered the terrain when he pulled up to the front of Beth and Howard's place. As he bridged the distance to the porch, he resolved not to prolong the visit this time. Exhausted by the hard pace he'd maintained the past few months, he pressed the doorbell, his eyes closing for a moment. When the door opened, he popped them open only to find he must have fallen asleep and was dreaming.

Kit grinned. "Come in. I was getting worried about you. Thankfully dinner is a soup that can stay on the burner for a while." She stepped to the side, gripping the door while she waited for him to enter.

Nate remained rooted to the porch. No words came to mind for several heartbeats, and then they assailed him. "Give your family my apologies. I'm no longer hungry."

He pivoted, but before he could take a step, Kit clutched his arm. "You can tell them yourself. They're at the cabin eating dinner."

He made the mistake of glancing over his shoulder at her. His heartbeat pounded in his chest while his mouth went dry. "What's going on?"

"I want to talk to you, and I was afraid if I came to see you that you'd slam the door in my face. Howard and Beth thought since you come out to the ranch every Tuesday that I could use that time to let you know I've returned to Cimarron City. For good."

He stiffened and yanked his arm from her grasp. "Who are you trying to fool into believing that? Me? You? Your family?"

Pain flitted across her face, but he wouldn't allow himself to be softened by that. These past months he'd been running as fast as he could from the memory of her and had found he'd remained stationary. In love with a woman who couldn't commit to him.

"You have every right to be angry with me. I'm angry with myself that it took so long to figure out what I really want in life. What was more important to me than even ballet."

He turned to confront her, his arms straight at his sides while he opened and closed his hands. "Don't say it's me, because I won't believe you. Twice you left because of your career. I can't take a third time."

"Madame Zoe is staying in New York, and I'm taking over her dance academy."

"Congratulations. Now I'm leaving."

"Please don't."

He shook his head as he backpedaled away from her, then spun on his heel and stormed down the stairs. When he reached his truck, fury rampaged through him. He drove away and didn't look back.

When Kit entered the cabin after cleaning up all evidence of her planned dinner for two with Nate, her family was finishing up the dishes. Beth took one look at her and asked Howard and the children to go back to their house without her.

The second Kit sat on the couch, Lexie jumped in her lap, clearly sensing that something was wrong with Kit.

When everyone was gone but Beth, she eased down in the chair across from Kit. “Obviously it didn’t go well. I’m not surprised. Some men can be stubborn.”

“No, Nate has every right to walk away after what I did to him. I’m not sure I’ll ever show him that I’m ready to make a commitment to him. When I decided to be a ballet dancer, I put everything behind it. Now I want to put everything into our relationship, but nothing will work between us unless he’s willing to believe me.”

“Then maybe time will be the answer.”

“I hope he’ll at least forgive me for hurting him a second time.”

“I hope so, too.”

After Beth left, Kit combed her fingers through Lexie’s coat. Time she had—what she lacked was the confidence that it would be enough.

When Kit entered the Harris Animal Hospital, she wished she was seeing Nate under different circumstances. It couldn’t be helped, though. He was covering the weekend and Lexie was sick.

Emma showed her into the room.

"Does Nate know I'm here?" Kit asked, fear for Lexie and for seeing Nate for the first time in two months encasing her in a cold chill.

"Yes. He's finishing up with another dog and will be here shortly." Emma peeked into the dog carrier. "Poor Lexie. She doesn't look good."

"Yesterday she wouldn't eat and what she did she threw up. I was up with her part of the night and knew first thing this morning I would have to bring her in. Look at her eyes. They're red."

The door opened, and Nate entered the examination room. A stoic expression quickly turned to a worried one when he lifted Lexie out of the carrier. "What is happening with her?"

Kit quickly gave him a list of symptoms. "I have a sample of her vomit. I know that might help you diagnose her." She handed him a plastic bag.

"I'll keep her here and run some tests. I suspect it is CPV."

"What?"

"Canine parvovirus infection. If so, it's highly contagious."

The beating of Kit's heart was a slow throb. "She'll be okay, won't she? I can't lose her."

Nate's look softened, his gaze connecting with hers for the first time since he came into the room. "Survival rate is high if treated. I'll take good care of her and keep you informed."

She touched his arm. "Thank you. I know she'll be in good hands with you and the others here. Let me know as soon as possible if there are any updates. Call my cell. I'll be at the high school. Tonight is the dance academy's winter Christmas production."

"We know about it. Madi has been asking us all week if we're going to come," Emma said as she zipped up the dog carrier and gave it back to Kit.

"Are you going?" Kit shifted her gaze from Emma to Nate.

"Yes," Emma said, but Nate remained quiet.

Kit stood offstage in the high school auditorium, relieved that Lexie was in good hands with Nate. When he called earlier to tell her Lexie had a confirmed diagnosis of CPV, he reassured her he would take care of her pet. Just the sound of his voice telling her that had calmed her fears about Lexie.

Anna ended the final dance of the evening and took a bow to the audience's applause. The teenager would go far in the ballet world if she kept progressing as she was. Kit remembered her own performance at Anna's age when she really didn't realize what was in store for her.

She'd had her share of highs and lows. Some she'd been prepared for; others she hadn't. She would help Anna as much as she could, but the young girl would have to discover many things on her own.

All the students came back out and took a group bow, and then family and friends flooded the stage. She loved seeing the smiles on the young girls' faces.

"You should be out there with them."

Nate's deep voice floated to her, and she wondered if she was imagining it. Then she swept around and spied him in the shadows a few feet away.

"Lexie's okay, isn't she?"

He smiled. "Yes, or I wouldn't be here. I'll check on her before I go home. I didn't want to miss your debut with the dance academy. I've been following your progress for the past two months, mostly through Madi, who eagerly gave me updates whenever she came to the animal hospital."

"You have? But earlier today, you acted so..."

"Cold? A defense mechanism when I think of you. When you left in July, I had to come up with something, and when you came back in October, I was sure you would leave within the month. I don't know if you knew but Howard and Beth asked me to Thanksgiving dinner. I told them no."

"I know. I suggested it." The loneliness in the midst of her family on Thanksgiving had only convinced her how much of a mistake she'd made by leaving Nate last summer. "I shouldn't have left in July."

"I think I understand why you did. It's taken me a while to work my way through it. You were given a great opportunity to remain in the middle of work you love and understand. If you hadn't gone and tried it, you might have regretted not taking the chance. You tried to tell me that in July. All I could think about was the first time you and I broke up. I didn't see you for years."

"I want to be up front with you. I've told Gordon I will do one ballet a year for him for as long as he wants. I kept my apartment in New York, and when I need to, I can travel back and stay with my girlfriend, who is living there, while I do what I need to with the company."

Nate opened his mouth to say something.

Holding up her hand, Kit rushed to explain, "But I won't if you ask me not to. I won't lose you over that. I'll be doing a lot of choreographing with the dance academy so I won't really be giving it up, even if I don't return to New York."

He closed the distance between them and

took her into his embrace. "How long will you be there each year?"

"Long enough to work with the dancers on the steps. After that, I can fly back and forth if they need me any further. I'm planning to do it during the summer when the Summer Dance Academy is through. There's always a six-week break before the students start back in the fall." She cherished the feel of his arms around her. She felt as though she'd truly come home. "You can always come for some of the time. I'd love to show you the city."

He bent his head and whispered against her lips, "I love you. We'll be able to work this out." Then he kissed her. When he drew back, he added, "I know how much dance means to you and—"

She covered his mouth with her fingertips. "Let me set this straight right now. You will *always* come first in my life. I've discovered ballet is only a part of my life. You and any family we have will be my priority."

"Any family we have?"

"Well, that is, if you ask me to marry you and we both decide to have children."

He knelt on one knee. "Then let me make this official. Kit, will you marry me?"

She framed his face and gave him a long, lingering kiss, then murmured, "Yes."

# *Epilogue*

*A year and a half later*

Nate cradled Kit against his side as they stood on the boat circling the island of Manhattan. The wind caught Kit's loose long hair, and it danced between them. She glanced up at him, a smile spreading across her face and reaching deep into her eyes.

"Are you tired yet of being the tourist?" she asked, amusement dimpling her cheeks.

"Why? What do you have in mind, Mrs. Sterling?"

"A quiet night at the apartment, savoring our news."

Nate laid his hand flat over her stomach. "I can't think of anything better than that. Are you positive you're pregnant? I'm not dreaming, am I?"

"To be sure the pregnancy kit was right, I went to see my doctor yesterday before you arrived in the city. I didn't want to say anything until I was sure."

Nate faced her, locking his arms around her and hauling her against him. "You don't think we celebrated enough last night?"

"We can never celebrate enough when our dream's coming true. You'll make the best dad."

Nate whispered his mouth over hers and said against her lips, "And you, the best mom."

"Our home will be filled with love," she said between light kisses.

"And hope that anything is possible." Then Nate claimed her mouth, shouting to the world his love for this woman.

* * * * *